Lo Mein

Also by Robert Eringer:

Strike for Freedom!
Monaco Cool
Zubrick's Rock
Crinkum Crankum

Lo Mein

ROBERT ERINGER

CORINTHIAN
BOOKS

Mt. Pleasant, S.C.

This is a work of imagination. In the few cases where actual names are used, the related characters, incidents and dialog are entirely fictional and are not intended to depict any real people or events.

Copyright ©2000 by Robert Eringer

All rights reserved. No part of this book may be used or reproduced in any form whatsoever without permission, except in the case of brief quotations embodied in critical reviews and articles.

Publishers Cataloging-in-Publication Data
(Provided by Quality Books, Inc.)

Eringer, Robert.
Lo mein / by Robert Eringer — 1st ed.
p. cm.
LCCN: 99-68979
ISBN: 1-929175-14-0 (hbk.)
ISBN: 1-929175-22-1 (pbk.)

1. Painters—Fiction. 2. Mass murder—Fiction. I. Title

PS3555.R48L66 2000   813'.54
                           QBI99-500558

Corinthian Books
an imprint of
The Côté Literary Group
P. O. Box 1898
Mt. Pleasant, S.C. 29465-1898
(843) 881-6080
http: //www.corinthianbooks.com

*For Don Jesse,
my high school English teacher*

1

WILLARD STUKEY'S ART was not selling. Not one painting. Canvases tripled along his walls, an incessant reminder not of the artist's failure, but of *society's* failure to recognize artistic genius. Fifty rejections was all he would tolerate. After number fifty, Stukey had decided, he would take action—drastic action—to achieve the fame that was his due. Willard Stukey was not about to wait till he was dead to earn the recognition he so richly deserved.

After rejection number forty-five, Stukey began a countdown inside his Soho loft. His home-slash-studio wasn't actually in Soho, but on the cheap end of the Village; nor was it a loft, but a sub-level two-room apartment. "Soho loft" is what he told people who asked. It sounded right; it fit his image, as he imagined his image to be. Good PR.

The final insult—Rejection Number Fifty—came from the Ricco-Maresco Gallery on artsy Wooster Street. This outrage was compounded by Stukey having misrepresented himself as an *outsider* artist. That is to say, an artist with no formal art training, Soho's latest craze, incorporating patients from mental institutions and poor black southern folk who painted with mud and pigments from fruit and vegetables.

In fact, Stukey had trained his whole life to be an artist, attending several shi-shi art and design schools. As part of his image, Stukey could imagine oil paint running through his veins.

And now this. Not even good enough to be an *outsider*.

Stukey had contemplated the possibilities of drastic action over goblets of Pernod and water in his favorite hangout, the Temple Bar, on Lafayette Street, frequented, as it was, by New York's arterati; had already decided upon his new medium: killing people. But he hadn't yet decided on form. Form, he understood—the artist that he was—was everything.

Should he stalk and murder the gallery owners who had so callously (and stupidly!) rejected his masterpieces? Stukey had poured his blood and guts into the abstract, textured works. Would it not be poetic (no, artistic!) to paint his canvases with *their* blood and guts and brains? What did they really know about art anyway?

Inside the Temple Bar, over a goblet of Pernod and water—a stab at emulating Vincent van Gogh's proclivity for absinthe—Stukey re-read the brusque, two sentence dismissal from Ricco-Maresco, before re-examining his own theory of art: Good art stirred emotion. Maybe it made you laugh; maybe it made you cry. If he could not convince the established art community with his brush, he would do it with another, less refined instrument. And soon, everyone, everywhere, would talk about Willard Stukey. As an extension of this, art dealers would broker his paintings; collectors would buy and hang them prominently. And, ah, the derision that would greet those who once rejected his work!

Ultimately, Stukey rejected the notion of victimizing the art community. It was just too simplistic. And tasted of sour chardonnay.

No, Stukey needed to make a bigger statement. He was out to break records.

2

ARMED WITH A HECHLER & KOCH MPSKA4 9mm machine pistol and five thirty-round magazines, Willard Stukey boarded an Amtrak train at Penn Station. As the locomotive rolled south, he sketched the faces of those around him in the dining car. He would document this journey. He would document everything with pen-and-ink sketches. They'd need a whole friggin' museum to show his art by the time he was through!

Stukey disembarked twenty-three hours later in Jacksonville, Florida, and rented a compact car from Budget. He did a quick pencil sketch of Budget's interior office as a clerk processed paperwork.

Then Willard Stukey drove seventy miles down Interstate 95, hung a roscoe onto Interstate 4, and checked into the Buena Vista Palace Hotel, part of the large complex belonging to Walt Disney World.

Inside his twelfth floor room, Stukey sketched the scene of Downtown Disney Marketplace from his window: Kids dodging intermittent jets of water and, behind them, a faux mountain belonging to the Rain Forest Cafe. Every so often, the mountain eructed steam into the air; a tacky, simulated volcanic eruption.

Stukey flipped to the next page of his sketchbook and drew a picture of the four-pound-five-ounce, thirteen-inch instrument of death that sat upon his table. Stukey had purchased this killing machine for fifty-five hundred dollars in the back room of an army surplus store where he'd bought military fatigues—his getup of choice since arriving in Manhattan three years earlier.

A final smidgeon of shadow, and Stukey snapped a magazine into the weapon. He snugged it under his armpit, beneath an Avirex leather bomber jacket, and headed downstairs.

The unknown artist alighted from a taxi at the entrance to Disney World's Magic Kingdom Park, rode a shiny silver monorail to its gates and entered on a one-day pass. He strode past a cluster of costumed cartoon characters—ignoring their friendly waves of greeting—and cut around to Town Square, at the bottom of Main Street, U.S.A. A clocktower above City Hall displayed the time: 7:22.

This is where the planning ended and spontaneity began.

Art, according to Willard Stukey, could only be created spontaneously. He'd simply wander around. When inspiration struck, well, so would he, with a brush and palette of hard steel.

Stukey sort of knew what he wanted: the longest line. How else to break a record? Did they even keep track of this sort of thing in that Guinness book? He entered the Kodak Camera Center and, indifferent to a queue, strode to the counter.

"What's the most popular attraction?" he demanded.

"That would be Splash Mountain," a helpful clerk interrupted a transaction to reply.

"Where?"

"Frontierland. We got some free maps over there." The clerk helpfully pointed to a cardboard display.

Stukey grabbed a map, spread it over the counter and focused his eyes on Frontierland. Wordlessly, he turned and left. Social grace was not part of Stukey's persona. Who needed manners when you possessed artistic talent?

The artist strolled Main Street in no hurry, absorbing the carnival of color; an aroma of popcorn—and the sound of a horn. It blared at him. Stukey whipped around. A trolley filled with passengers wanted to get by and he was on the track. The trolley driver smiled.

Stukey had an impulse to do it then and there; to wipe the smile off that driver's ugly face. But he thought better of it. An artist, after all, did not react. He *created*—and only when the circumstances were just so. It was for others to react to *him*.

Stukey stepped aside and veered left, a path that led through Adventureland. He walked on, glancing this way and that. In another minute he was there. The long line for Splash Mountain doubled, tripled, even quadrupled in some spots. A sign near its end informed guests of a one-hour-and-twenty-minute wait for this attraction.

Stukey walked the length of the queue, fingering the trigger of the killing machine beneath his jacket. No, it wouldn't do. An artist had to be careful about choosing the right canvas, about not being influenced by false inspiration. Move on, move on.

Stukey doubled back around the lake circling Tom Sawyer's Island. A riverboat passed by. He paused by the Haunted Mansion, then roamed into Fantasyland. Here, hundreds of toddlers waited their turn to enter It's a Small World and Peter Pan's Flight, among many attractions designed for small children.

No, no, no–the angles were all wrong. It wouldn't do. Maybe he needed a bite to eat, calm his nerves?

Stukey ducked into Pinocchio Village Haus Restaurant, took his place in line and ordered a smoked turkey sandwich. He nabbed a Bavarian-style wooden table and chair and chomped on bland poultry, his gaze focusing upon a mural of a fairy princess with a magic wand. "When you wish upon a star," it read, "all your dreams come true."

"Yup," Stukey muttered under his breath, "that's what I got in mind."

The artist stood, strode past Dumbo the Flying Elephant, around Cinderella's Golden Carrousel, and through Cinderella's Castle–a route that spilled him into a circle at the top end of Main Street, near a life-sized statue of Walt Disney and his buddy Mickey Mouse.

Epiphany!

And with it, the inspiration Stukey sought on his unique *artiste's* wavelength: A crowd had formed on both sides of Main Street, U.S.A. It ran two sides and, fanning out at both ends, had taken the shape of an hourglass.

This was form.

Nearby, a Disney employee swept the path.

"What's going on?" Stukey motioned a shoulder at the sea of people before him.

"The Electric Parade," said the gawky youth. "It starts at nine."

"What's the time now?" Stukey demanded. He did not carry a timepiece. Time was unimportant to artists of his calibre. At least until now.

The youth checked his wristwatch. "Twenty of."

Stukey smiled. The Disneyland Electric Parade! Energy! Emotion! Art!

Inspired at last, Stukey sat upon a bench and sketched Cinderella's Castle.

At nine p.m. sharp, the parade began. Stukey positioned himself behind a quadrupled line of spectators, next to a J. M. Smucker display window filled with jarred jams and jellies. He stood on the tips of his old, paint-splattered brogues to catch a glimpse of the living, breathing cartoon mosaic: elaborate floats that carried Snow White and the Seven Dwarfs, Beauty and the Beast, Winnie the Pooh, Peter Pan, and Captain Hook.

Colored lights pulsated wildly to drumbeats from high school bands interspersed between floats.

Stukey glanced left and right for a final bout of afflatus that would entice him to artistry. He found it in the climactic float: Mickey and Minnie Mouse. They were holding hands, waving, blowing kisses.

What a statement!

Stukey waded into the spectators, elbowing and footstepping.

"Hey," protested a big man wearing Mickey Mouse ears. "Watch it, bud."

This kind of insolence deserved the first brush stroke. Stukey extracted the Hechler & Koch MPSKA4 machine pistol from his jacket and shoved its barrel into the big man's bulging stomach. "Watch *this*, bud!" He squeezed the trigger and discharged two rounds.

The big man fell backwards, arms flapping, countenance contorting. He collapsed dramatically into those behind him, seeping blood and bile.

Stukey stepped over the curb, into the street. He pointed his weapon at Mickey and Minnie and let it rip.

Within seven seconds, thirty rounds were discharged. Stukey dug into his jacket pocket, retrieved a new magazine and clipped it into place. He commenced another round of firing as he sprinted down Main Street, shooting at spectators on both sides of the road.

Many of those who did not see the artist at work believed the firework show had begun, and looked to the sky.

Stukey let the second clip drop from his machine pistol and replaced it with a third. This he used to blow an opening through the crowd assembled on Town Square.

Behind Stukey, a stampede was underway, people running in all directions, trampling small children to escape the slaughter. Main Street's gutters ran red and gooey with blood.

Artwork complete, Stukey snugged the weapon into his jacket, between armpit and hugging waistband, and heaved himself into a wave of people routed toward the front gates.

Outside the park, Stukey ascended an escalator to the monorail station. Within a minute, a train glided in. Stukey stepped aboard, nabbed a seat and reached under his jacket for the sketch pad he always kept tucked into his pants, at the small of his back. Calmly, he pencil-sketched the interior of the train, listening to the frantic ravings of other passengers about the slaughter that had just transpired inside the Magic Kingdom.

Stukey alighted at Walt Disney World's Contemporary Hotel. He strolled through it, absorbing the shock waves as word of his product reverberated within its walls.

Outside, he climbed into a taxi. "Buena Vista Palace," he said, in a voice as serene as the Polynesian lagoon nearby.

3

In BURBANK, CALIFORNIA, Disney chairman Michael Eisner was concluding a routine business meeting when an ashen-faced aide rushed into his spacious office overlooking Disney Studios. She whispered into Eisner's ear.

Blood drained from the chairman's face. He plucked a remote from his desk and illuminated his large-screen TV with CNN. A Breaking News segment was reporting a mass murder at Disney World.

Of all the things that could happen to his entertainment empire, this was Michael Eisner's worst nightmare. The lawsuits alone could potentially haunt his company for the rest of his life. The damage to Disney's image would be irreparable.

Eisner's phone rang. A police detective from the Orlando Police Department needed to speak with him urgently.

"Put him through," snapped Eisner.

"Mr. Eisner? I'm Detective Wick, Homicide. A terrorist attack of some kind has just occured in your park."

"I'm watching CNN," replied Eisner.

"We need to know if you've received letters from anyone threatening to do such a thing."

"We receive letters from kooks on a weekly basis," replied an anguished Eisner. "I never see them. They're channeled directly to security."

"Maybe I should talk to your security chief?"

"Consider us both on our way." Eisner put down the phone, paused a moment, eyes closed. Then he began snapping orders to ready the Gulfstream jet for immediate departure.

4

WILLARD STUKEY RACED up Interstate 75, past Gainesville, toward Atlanta. In his wake he'd left a landscape of hell. Scores of ambulances were needed to cart the dead and wounded to area hospitals. Most of the casualties were young children, victims of adults intent on fleeing the scene. Good samaritans lined up to heed the call for much needed blood.

Thirty-two deaths had already been confirmed. At least seventy-nine others were hospitalized with gunshot wounds and other serious injuries. The dead included two Disney employees costumed as Mickey and Minnie Mouse.

This is what Stukey learned from his car radio.

"I killed Mickey Mouse?" Stukey shook his head, incredulous. "Now *that's* art!"

He pulled into a rest stop, parked and retrieved his sketchbook from the backseat. Every aspect of this live art experience had to be recorded, including a stretch of Florida interstate.

5

ORLANDO'S POLICE DEPARTMENT closed the Magic Kingdom Park and sealed off two acres of crime scene with yellow tape. A homicide team combed every inch of Main Street, collecting empty shells and two spent magazine cartridges. They packed everything into plastic baggies for transfer by air to the FBI forensics lab at Quantico, Virginia.

In a terse, prepared statement to the news media, which had rambunctiously assembled outside park gates, a police spokesman asked that everyone who had witnessed the crime make themselves known to the police—particularly those who had been photographing the parade with still or video cameras.

6

JEFF DALKIN OCCUPIED a window table inside Soup Burg, an eatery on the corner of Madison Avenue and Seventy-third Street in Manhattan. He was tucked into the house specialty, a Smother Burger Deluxe–prime sirloin smothered in fried onions, mushrooms and Muenster cheese, lettuce and tomtato–when his cellular phone whistled.

Dalkin flicked it open, mouth full. "Yeah–what?"

"I need you," said a voice that Dalkin recognized; a prized, occasional client.

"I'm there." Dalkin swallowed. "Where?"

"Orlando. Where are you now?"

"Soup Burg."

"*Where?*"

"New York City," said Dalkin. "Niggers and kikes. Fuck, sorry, I. . ."

"Can you get to Orlando today?" This was more of a demand than a question. "Our Yacht Club Resort."

"I'm there, boss. Blow a fart. No . . . ah, fuck it." Dalkin disconnected his phone, wiped his plate clean and settled the tab.

"Thanks, Mr. Willis," said the waiter.

"I'm not Bruce W-W-Willis," said Dalkin, who, in fact, looked exactly like the famous thespian, right down to his bizarre hairline and idiosyncratic facial expressions.

"Yeah, right." The waiter rolled his eyes.

Five taxi cabs dived at Dalkin as he stepped over the curb on Madison Avenue and raised an arm. He climbed into the nearest one.

"Where to, Brucie?" asked the excited cabbie.

"LaGuardia."

The cab raced east to FDR, over the Triboro Bridge, into Queens.

"Can you call your dispatch," said Dalkin, "find out what airline's flying to Orlando this afternoon?"

"Sure, Bruce, whatever you want, man."

Dalkin smugged to himself. This kind of attention was one of the benefits of being mistaken for a famous movie star.

The cabbie did his thing. "US Airways," he said, "at three-twenty."

Dalkin alighted at the US Airways terminal and strode to the ticket counter.

An African-American ticket clerk did a double-take. "Mr. Willis? How can I help you?"

"I need to get on your three-twenty to Orlando. And I'm not Bruce W-W-Willis." Dalkin produced his driver's license and American Express card.

The clerk perused Dalkin's identification. "Jeff Dalkin?" She smiled. "That's cute. But you could get into trouble using a phony license," she whispered. "And I could get in trouble accepting this as picture ID."

"I *am* Jeff Dalkin."

The clerk nodded, unsure, and processed a ticket. "Did you have a pleasant stay in New York?" she asked.

"I live in New York. Niggers and kikes. Oh, shit."

The clerk's facial features froze in horror.

"I didn't mean . . . black boobs. Christ, never mind." Dalkin found it futile to explain his syndrome: Tourette's. He grabbed the boarding pass from her hand and galloped off.

The flight was already boarding when Dalkin reached the gate. He strode onto the aircraft, glancing this way and that. He did not like what he saw. At row ten he whirled around to face the flight attendant, five yards away. "What kind of plane is this?" he called out anxiously.

"A DC-nine," she replied.

"A *what?*"

"DC-nine."

"That makes it what, about thirty years old?" Dalkin's face twitched.

"Every plane we fly meets our safety standards," said the flight attendant, "whatever its age."

"Safe isn't the only problem, honey," said Dalkin. "These old bastards make one helluva racket. And your ears pop like champagne corks. I didn't know US Air was a cut-rate airline."

"We are not cut-rate," huffed the flight attendant.

"Could've fooled me, honey. Bargs. I'm outta here."

The pilot poked his head through the cabin door in time to see Dalkin exit. "Was that Bruce Willis?" he asked.

7

EIGHTEEN HOURS AFTER his one-man blitz on Disney World, Willard Stukey reached the outskirts of Bardstown, his native Kentucky. The artist's original plan had been to return to New York City where, he assumed, capture awaited him—and with it, a full examination, a full *appreciation*, of his numerous painted canvases. But after grabbing eight hours kip at a roadside Days Inn motel, Stukey had developed a craving for burgoo. And there was only one state in the whole world that prepared this delicacy on which the artist had been bred.

Stukey was good and hungry when he pulled into the parking lot of the Blue Grass Diner. As far as Stukey was concerned, this was where the best burgoo in the world was stewed. He pulled off a pair of Oakley frogskins and stroked his three-day beard. When they came for him, this was how he wanted to look on the cover of *Time* magazine. "The artist who killed Mickey Mouse." That was his caption of preference.

Stukey nailed a booth.

A matronly waitress approached with a menu.

"I know what I want." Stukey waved the menu away. "Burgoooooo."

"We don't do burgoo no more," said the waitress, matter-of-fact.

"What do you mean, no burgoo?" Stukey was stupefied.

"Haven't you heard about the scare?"

"What are you talking about?" Stukey scratched his itchy beard. "What scare?"

"Mad squirrel disease. *Nobody* eats burgoo no more."

"Mad what?" Stukey could scarcely believe his ears.

"Mad squirrel disease. It's a virus in squirrel brains. Can't eat 'em no more. So no burgoo. We got possum. You want possum?"

8

JEFF DALKIN MADE IT to Orlando on American Airlines, arriving at Disney's Yacht Club Resort just before nine p.m. He was escorted to the fifth-floor Admiral's Suite.

Inside, Michael Eisner was pacing. "Ah, there you are," he greeted Dalkin solemnly. "Sit down."

Dalkin perched himself on an ottoman inside the suite's octagonal parlor, which enjoyed a sweeping panorama of a mock 1930s Atlantic coast boardwalk.

"I assume you know why you're here?" Eisner had bags beneath his eyes from lack of sleep.

"It has to do with yesterday's . . . ?"

"Correct," Eisner interjected. "We have reason to think CNN is in possession of an amateur videotape that shows Mickey and Minnie Mouse being gunned down by a madman. We cannot allow this tape to be shown to the public. It would be devastating to our image. Look at this." Eisner held up that morning's *Orlando Sentinel.* The headline, embazoned in bold, read: *Maniac Murders Mickey.* Eisner shook his head. "This is bad, very bad."

Dalkin nodded solemnly.

"I want you to get it back," said Eisner.

"Excuse me?"

"The videotape." Eisner snapped his fingers twice. "Get it back from CNN."

"If CNN—maggots and turds—has it," said Dalkin, "why haven't they already shown it?"

"Because our lawyers have injuncted them. Infringement of our Mickey trademark. But CNN's fighting it. And it's just a matter of days, maybe hours, before some judge reverses our injunction." Eisner slammed his right hand into his left fist. "I want it back!"

"How?"

"Money. Whatever it costs. It's your job to ensure that not one frame of a fallen Mickey Mouse appears on TV, or in magazines or newspapers, or in the tabloids, which, incidentally, are offering big money."

Dalkin whistled. "As I understand it," he said, "*Minnie* Mouse was also murdered."

"*Not* Minnie Mouse!" Eisner barked. "An actor in a Minnie Mouse costume!"

"Got it." Dalkin scribbled with his pen into a pocket notebook. "And I thought you were calling me in to help find the killer."

"Not necessary. They know who he is."

"Has that come out in the news yet?"

"No." Eisner shook his head. "My security chief was a bigwig at the FBI."

"The Bureau? Back-assed bowel-offs."

Eisner cocked a brow.

"Excuse me, sir. I'm trying to keep my problem under control, but certain words. . . ."

"Never mind," snapped Eisner. "The murderer is from New York. We got the FBI into it on the presumption of interstate flight."

Jeff Dalkin flew Eisner's private jet out of Executive Airport in Orlando to Atlanta. He turned up at One CNN Center nine-thirty the next morning.

"I need to see the producer in charge of the Breaking News story on the Mickey murder manhunt," Dalkin told the receptionist.

That is what CNN was calling it: *The Mickey Murder Manhunt*.

The receptionist focused on Dalkin's looks, not his words.

"Bu . . . Bu . . . Bruce Willis?" she stammered

"If that's what it takes," said Dalkin.

"What, uh, *who* do you need to see?"

"Whoever's running coverage of the Mickey murder manhunt. Sweater full of kajoobies. Ohhhh, shit." Dalkin put his right hand over his mouth. "I didn't mean . . . ."

The receptionist grinned wickedly as she picked up the phone and shared words with someone.

Dalkin hoped it wasn't security.

"He'll be with you in a few minutes, Mr. Willis." She patted her honey blonde hair. "Would you like a cup of coffee or something?"

"No thanks. Big bodacious bazongas bouncing over my blow-torch. Shit, goddammit!" Dalkin blushed purple, mortified by his Tourettic outburst.

Five minutes later, a balding, middle-aged man approached Dalkin. "Mr. Willis?" He stepped forward and

shook Dalkin's hand. "Hugh Scrupula. What can I do for you?" This question was laced with puzzlement.
"Michael Ei-yi-yi-yisner sent me," whispered Dalkin. He glanced around at gawking passersby. "Can we take this to your office?"
"Oh, of course, sorry." Scrupula led Dalkin through the vast newsroom to his corner cubicle. "Please, have a seat."
The two men sat and regarded each other within a cozy ensemble of stuffed furniture.
"So what's the latest?" asked Dalkin.
"We think the FBI is onto someone," said Scrupula. "but they're keeping it close to their chest."
"It's true," Dalkin smirked like Bruce Willis. "The Bureau–butt-wipe bowel-offs from bargsterville–they know who the killer is."
Scrupula flinched, then leaned forward. "Do you have a name?"
"Yep," said Dalkin. "I want to make you a deal, Mr. . . Scrupula?"
Scrupula nodded. He plucked a black leather billfold from his trouser pocket, extracted a business card and handed it to Dalkin. "Call me Hugh."
"Thanks, Hugh, butt-face," Dalkin slid the card into his shirt pocket. "You'll excuse me. I don't carry cards."
"You don't need one!" laughed Scrupula.
"Exactly right. Now, here's the deal," said Dalkin. "I'm prepared to reveal to you the identity of the man the Bureau–baloney-beating bargsters–the Bureau's looking for. In return, I'd like you to give me the amateur videotape of the murder and put an end to the litigation between us."

Scrupula struck a deep pose.

"Am I talking to the right guy?" said Dalkin. "Do you have the power to deal?"

Scrupula nodded. "I can deal. But I need more."

"Like what?"

"Eisner hasn't said a word in public since the event," said Scrupula, ever the newsman. "We want the first interview with him."

"Can I use a phone?" asked Dalkin.

"Use mine." Scrupula got up, pointed to his desk. "I'll wait outside."

Dalkin sat at the desk, touch-keyed a direct line to room 5157, the Admiral's Suite at Disney's Yacht Club Resort. He connected to Eisner and laid out the deal.

"Do it," snapped Eisner.

Dalkin put the phone down and poked his head out of Scrupula's office. "Hugh? The boss–blow a fart–agreed."

Scrupula summoned his secretary to follow them into his office. He dictated a memorandum of intent, asked her to type it forthwith and prepare two copies for signing.

The secretary returned a few minutes later.

Dalkin signed his own name over *Bruce Willis for Michael Eisner.*

"What's this?" said Scrupula, poised to pen his own signature.

"My name."

"Dalkin?"

"That's right. Jeff Dalkin."

"But you're Bruce Willis," said Scrupula.

Dalkin shook his head. "I'm Jeff Dalkin. I never said I'm Bruce W-W-Willis."

"But you look exactly like. . . ." Scrupula narrowed his eyes, incredulous.

"Yeah, everyone tells me that."

"Jeez. Have you ever thought of getting a job in movies as Bruce Willis's double?"

"I don't have to," grinned Dalkin. "Everywhere I go I'm B-B-Bruce's double. I never have to wait in lines at restaurants, and I've had more babes than I can keep track of."

"Amazing." Scrupula shook his head. He crossed out *Bruce Willis* on both copies of the memo, printed *Jeff Dalkin* and initialed the change. He hesitated. "Do you think I could have a word with Mr. Eisner for confirmation?"

Dalkin shrugged. "Sure." He picked up the phone, reconnected to Eisner. "This CNN turds-and-maggots guy, Hugh butt-face Scrupple. . .? Scruple. . .?"

"Scrupula," said Scrupula.

"Scrupula. He wants a word with you." Dalkin handed the phone over.

"Mr. Eisner?"

"Yeah."

"I just want to be sure that Mr. . . ." he looked at Dalkin. ". . . Dalkin fully represents you."

"He does."

"Okay, thanks." Scrupula returned the phone to Dalkin.

"Thanks, boss," said Dalkin. "Blow a fart. Sorry, it's the word *boss.* Blow a fart. Goddamit! Goodbye."

Scrupula shook his head, awed. Maybe he should finally take a sabbatical and write that novel he'd been kicking around. He handed the documents to Dalkin for his own initials. "You keep one, I'll keep one. So," Scrupula smiled. "Who are they looking for?"

Dalkin shook his head. "First I need the videotape."

Scrupula shrugged. "I'll be right back." He returned four minutes later and handed Dalkin a Sony camcorder cassette.

"Let's watch it." Dalkin gestured at Scrupula's TV/VCR set-up.

"Why not." Scrupula plunked the tape into his VCR.

They watched as a man wearing olive-green fatigues and a leather bomber jacket jumped into the street and fired a machine pistol directly at Mickey and Minnie Mouse. Then the camera swung upwards and away as the camera operator fled the scene.

It was only eight seconds, but it was awesome.

"Here's your problem as I see it." It was Scrupula who finally spoke. "There were probably twenty people with video cameras close enough to get this." He shook his head. "You've got your work cut out for you. So . . ." He fused his eyes into Dalkin's. "Who are the FBI looking for?"

9

WILLARD STUKEY HAD JUST passed Lancaster, Pennsylvania, en route to New York City, when he heard his name over the car radio.

"CNN has reported a break in the Mickey Murder Manhunt," announced a newsreader. "The FBI have a suspect. They're looking for Willard Stukey, a failed artist from New York City. . . ."

Everything else after that was just a bunch of blah-blahs to Stukey's ears.

Sure, he expected them to figure out it was he, Willard Stukey, *Artiste*, who had expressed himself so dramatically —so artistically! That, indeed, was the whole point of this exhibition of live art, was it not? But what was this *failed* crap? He hadn't failed. On the contrary—and Stukey was very much the contrarian—he had *succeeded.* If he hadn't succeeded, why was his name such a big deal right now? They just didn't get it. Maybe he'd just have to spell it out for them.

Seething, Stukey veered off Route 222 into Reading,

an old railroad town known for its cut-rate factory outlets. He did not have a shopping spree in mind.

Stukey parked in a metered space outside the *Reading Eagle* on Penn Street. With the killing machine tucked beneath his bomber jacket, loaded with a fresh magazine, Stukey crossed the road and entered Jimmy Kramer's Peanut Bar.

"You got a phone in here?" he barked at the first person he ran into, a short, rotund manager.

"Back there."

Stukey stalked to the rear of the restaurant, picked up the public phone and tapped zero.

"Operator."

"This is an emergency," said Stukey. "I need you to connect me to CNN."

"I'm sorry, sir," the operator replied. "I can only connect you to police, fire, or ambulance."

"Okay. I hear you. Then make it a collect call."

"To what number?"

"If I knew that," said Stukey, "I'd dial it myself, goddammit."

"You need information?" The operator didn't wait for an answer.

"City and state," said an automated voice.

"I need CNN's number," said Stukey.

"Where are they?" asked a human voice.

"Sonofabitch. As far as I can tell, they're everywhere," said Stukey. "Just give me the best number you got. No, don't give it to me. Connect me. A collect call."

"From who?"

"From Willard Stukey, *successful* artist."

"Hold on."

Stukey held, marching in place to exercise legs stiff from driving.

The operator came back on. "You may go ahead, sir."

"Hello?" said Stukey.

"CNN. How may I direct your call?"

"News," said Stukey. "Big news."

Hugh Scrupula was conducting a telephone conference with three field producers, strategizing that afternoon's Breaking News coverage, when his secretary burst in on him.

"I'm sorry, Hugh, but there's a man on the phone who claims he's Willard Stukey."

Scrupula looked up. "Did you say *Stukey?*"

"Yes. I thought you might want to be interrupted for this."

"Are you sure it's not a crank?"

"He's very insistent."

"Okay," said Scrupula. "Put him through."

The secretary hurried back to her desk.

"Hold on guys," Scrupula switched lines to address his caller. "This is Hugh Scrupula."

"So what," shot Stukey. "I'm looking for the bozo who called me a failed artist."

"Who is this?" Scrupula demanded.

"Willard Stukey."

"Are you the Stukey who shot Mickey Mouse at Walt Disney World?"

"There's only one Willard Stukey. He's a *successful* artist. And I'm him, goddammit."

"How do I know you're not some crank?"

"Who cares what you know," said Stukey. "Who are you anyway?"

"I'm senior producer in charge of Breaking News."

"Sounds like you clowns at CNN are breaking wind to me. Who said I'm a failed artist?"

"Mr. Stukey, where are you calling from?"

"You can call me Willard. I'm at a public phone."

"Where?"

"That's my business," said Stukey. "Your business is to get the facts straight. And as far as I can tell, you're fucking it all up."

"No need to swear Mister, uh, Willard."

"No? Would you swear if I called you a failed news producer?"

Scrupula did not reply.

"Have you ever seen my paintings?" demanded Stukey.

"No. I . . . where . . . ?"

"So, if you and your news clowns haven't seen my paintings, how can you judge me to be a failed artist–and report that on TV? I should sue your ass for libel!"

"But that's your reputation," said Scrupula.

"My reputation? What the hell do you know about my reputation?"

"We've been checking, interviewing your neighbors, Willard. Your paintings don't sell."

"Did van Gogh sell any paintings?" Stukey hollered. "Would you call van Gogh a failed artist, you goddamn moron?!"

Scrupula's secretary rushed in with Willard Stukey's vital statistics, retrieved from newsroom data bases.

"Willard, just so I can be sure it's really you, could you

tell me your social security number?"

"Real artists don't allow themselves to be numbered," said Stukey.

"Okay, how about your date of birth?"

Stukey recited month, day and year.

"Okay, I believe it's really you."

"Gee, like, thank's a lot," said Stukey. "Now can we get serious?"

"Why did you go on a shooting rampage at Walt Disney World?" Scupula's tone was sharp.

"What are you, my grade school principal? That was a live art exhibition. You think I'm gonna to wait 'til I'm dead like van Gogh to get the recognition I deserve?"

"That's why you did it? For attention?"

"I'd rather be recognized a great artist behind bars than be ridiculed a free man. That's an original quote, by the way."

Scrupula had a new thought. "Willard, can I put you on the air?"

"On TV? When?"

"Right now. In a minute or two. I'd like to connect you to Lou Waters, our anchor, and take you live."

"Fine. But first he's got to take back this *failed* shit."

"What do you want him to say?"

"Say something like, Willard Stukey, the famous artist, is willing to say a few words."

"But you're not a famous artist."

"I am now," growled Stukey.

Scrupula's hands trembled as he connected to CNN's central control booth. "I have Willard Stukey on the phone

. . . yep, *that* Willard Stukey. He's actually admitting, actually, he's *boasting* about his shooting rampage at Disney World. He's standing by to go live. Tell Lou. I'll put Stukey through to his hotline in thirty seconds."

Lou Waters was advised through an earpiece receiver that his phone would ring and Willard Stukey would be on the other end.

"The suspect in the Mickey Murder Manhunt–Willard Stukey–is on the phone with CNN," Waters announced to his viewers. "We're going to bring that to you now." The phone rang. Waters picked it up. "Mr. Stukey? Are you there?"

"Am I where?" said Stukey.

"Where are you?" asked Waters.

"None of your goddamn business!" snapped Stukey. "Have you told your viewers that you mis-reported my reputation?"

"Uh, you mean you deny shooting anyone at Walt Disney World?"

"No! Course I did that, you moron! I'm talking about saying I'm a failed artist without even looking at my paintings. If you saw my work, you'd say I'm a *successful* artist. A *great* artist!"

"So you did murder Mickey Mouse?"

"Damn right I did," replied Stukey. "But that's not the point."

"Not the point?"

"It sure ain't. This killing stuff is a just footnote."

"How can you. . . ?"

"That was a live art exhibition, something I'm doin' because the art community is too fucked up to understand greatness."

"But you have murdered innocent people," said Lou Waters.

"Why are you so hung up on that?" said Stukey.

"And Mickey Mouse," said Waters. "He is the most popular icon of our times."

"*Was.*" A new impulse synapsed through Stukey's brain. "This is just the beginning, guy. Donald Duck is next. And after that, Goofy. And after Goofy, Snow White, and all seven of those fucking dwarfs. If my demands are not met."

"Demands? We're not aware of any demands," said Waters.

"I didn't have any until you bozos called me a failed artist. Now I got a few. I'm a successful artist, you got that? And to prove it, I'm going to have an exhibition at MoMA."

"Where?"

"The Museum of Modern Art, in New York City."

"Really? When?"

"It better be soon. That's demand number one. I want my paintings exhibited at MoMA, for everyone to see. Number two, the *New York Times* has to review my show. A whole page review with samples of my best work. Until that happens, I'm gonna keep knocking off Disney characters."

"To whom have you made these demands?"

"I'm making them to you, you idiot, right now, for everyone to hear. If the FBI knows who I am, they must know my address in New York City. That's where my paintings are. I expect to be elsewhere, myself. But I leave it to them to get my paintings over to MoMA, pronto. After my paintings are exhibited for one full week and the *New York Times* reviews my show, that's when my demonstration of live art will end, and I'll give myself up."

"But Mr. Stukey," said CNN's anchor. "Why Disney?"

"Why not Disney? It represents the crass commercialization of art. Say, aren't you that cloned newscaster who looks like a robot?"

"What?" said Waters. "No, that was Linden Soles."

"Gotta go," said Stukey.

"Go where?"

"See ya–bye." Stukey put down the phone and strode through Jimmy Kramer's.

Patrons were grouped at the bar, watching Lou Waters on CNN, yakking into a dead line. "Mr. Stukey, are you there? Mr. Stukey?"

A new sense of purpose had overtaken the artist. He looked down at the fatigues he'd been wearing for five days straight. Time for a make-over.

"Do you have a Brooks Brothers in this town?" he stopped to ask the manager.

"Better. We have a Brooks Brothers *outlet*."

Stukey took directions, returned to his car, and drove to an outlet complex of strip malls in the old part of the city.

At Brooks Brothers, Stukey bought a navy-blue suit (size 38 regular), two white button-down oxfords (size 15-33), and a striped silk tie. He paid with cash, peeling nine Ben Franklins from a thick wad of hundreds, the balance of what was bequeathed him by a favorite aunt, the only one of his relatives who believed in his artistic talent.

While Brookies tailored his suit trousers, Stukey strolled to a Cole-Haan outlet and purchased a pair of shiny black wingtips and some black socks. At Lenscrafters he bought a pair of RayBan Wayfarers. And at a luggage outlet he found a stiff garment bag for carrying his new look.

Then Stukey took a cheap room at an outlet-catering motel. He bathed, shaved his stubble, and gave himself a haircut, chopping at the stringy ends over his ears and neck, and slicking back everything else with Brylcreme.

Stukey suited himself and donned his RayBans.

Whoa! The bathroom mirror reflected a Man in Black.

Stukey stowed his duffle of old clothes in the Budget rental car's trunk, returned to Jimmy Kramer's, and sat down for thick-cut pork chops and sauerkraut.

10

MICHAEL EISNER WAS apoplectic with fury when Jeff Dalkin reappeared in his spacious suite at Disney's Yacht Club Resort.

"Can you believe," Eisner exploded, "that CNN would give that . . . that *murdering* bastard a platform for saying that he's going to keep gunning down Disney characters if his absurd demands are not met?!"

"Live television," shrugged Dalkin. "They have no control."

"Of all the irresponsible. . . !"

"At least we got the videotape." Dalkin waved the cartridge. "But it won't solve the problem."

Eisner sat down and glumly rested his head in his hands. "What now?"

"Hugh butt-face Scrupula, the Breaking News producer for CNN—turds and maggots, sorry—reckons there are at least a dozen different versions of this floating around. He has pledged not to be the first to show videotape of Mickey Mouse getting blown away. But that won't stop the networks, or local stations, from acquiring and airing videotape from other amateur video cameramen who were on the scene. And if that happens, CNN—turds and maggots—will consider itself free to license and re-broadcast to the world."

"I'll sue!" Eisner protested. "Our customers are permitted to take photographs of our characters, but they cannot use those images for commercial purposes. It is infringement of our trademark."

"You don't think the First Amendment applies?"

"CNN, the networks, even local stations are commercial businesses."

"You'll spend millions—blow me—on litigation and the damage will already be done," said Dalkin. "I've got a better idea."

"What idea?" Eisner snapped his fingers.

"Let's beat everyone in the media—pomegranate-pounders—to whatever videotape exists. Disney should offer a reward to anyone who turns in original videotape of the offending scene."

Eisner looked up. "Of course, of course! A reward! We'll *buy* everything!"

"And I'll tell you how we do it," added Dalkin. "You'll make the announcement on CNN—turds and maggots. Let's beat the media—pomegranate-pounding pricks—at their own game."

"How—?"

"You promised them an exclusive interview," said Dalkin. "So let's get it on. You'll announce the reward on live TV. One million dollars. Blow me. Offer one million dollars— blow me—for the return of each and every amateur video. If that doesn't do it, it wasn't meant to be done."

"But what if these amateurs make copies from the originals?"

"I'm not a lawyer—lying labonzas," hissed Dalkin, "but it seems to me you should make each recipient of the reward sign a contract stating that no copies have been made, and if any turn up, not only must the reward be returned, but they're liable to a one million dollar—blow me—penalty."

"Brilliant," said Eisner. "We'll do a CNN interview right here, in this suite. Next item. How close is the FBI to catching this Stukey guy? It's not possible he could actually strike again, is it?"

"You mean murder Donald Duck?"

"Donald Duck cannot be murdered!" snapped Eisner.

"I'll check with a former colleague at the Bureau—big-assed baloney-beating butt-licks. See what they know. Meantime, you might consider tightening security at your theme parks."

11

WILLARD STUKEY WATCHED the passing Pennsylvania landscape through the grimy window of a Greyhound bus. The sun had already set ahead of him, and the rumble of the bus, along with an endless stretch of interstate, slowly mesmerized the artist into a light doze.

Stukey had left his car in the Peanut Bar's parking lot, walked a mile to the bus station and boarded the first bus out. That was the plan: first bus out. Let destiny be his guide. He'd always wanted to travel that way.

About the same time—early evening—a Gulfstream touched down at Reagan-National Airport in Washington, D.C. Dalkin, who had persuaded the Disney chairman to gas up the corporate jet for his use, disembarked.

A chauffeur led Dalkin from the terminal to a beige Lincoln Towncar parked in the hourly lot.

"Foong Lin," said Dalkin, sinking into plush leather. "It's a Chinese–midget mutherfucks–restaurant in Bethesda."

The driver shot a nervous sideways glance. "Are you shooting a movie here, Mr. Willis?"

Dalkin grunted.

R. James Cloverland, assistant director of the FBI's criminal division, was nursing a bottle of Hsing-Tao beer inside the bustling restaurant. He looked like a marshal from the wild west in his cowboy boots and weathered face with thick handlebar moustache.

Dalkin looked around, glimpsed his old Bureau buddy and strode over.

The two men hugged, sat down.

"So," said Dalkin. "How's everything at the Bureau–butt-faced ball-less baloney-blowers!"

Patrons at neighboring tables recoiled in horror.

Cloverland put his hands over his ears. "Some things never change."

"You know I can't help it," said Dalkin. "Certain words set me off. Bureau–baboon-blowing butt-holes–happens to be one of them."

"I'm not surprised." Cloverland sunk into his chair to escape attention.

"*I'm* surprised I did fifteen years at that fucking institution," said Dalkin. "And that *wasn't* Tourette's."

"Easy boy. I assume the reason you're here is because you need assistance from that fucking institution, as you put it."

Dalkin nodded. "I'm working for Michael Ei . . . Ei . . . Ei-yi-yi-yi. . . ." Dalkin sang like a Mexican mariachi. "Ei-yi-yeisner."

Cloverland whistled softly. "You landed on your feet

with a client like that."

"It took a while." Dalkin hailed a passing oriental waitress. "Let me have one of those Chinese–midget mutherfucks—uh, one of those beers." He pointed to Cloverland's bottle. "And let's order some grub."

Cloverland gazed at the blackboard specials above him. "Hot Hunan shredded beef with spicy sauce," he said.

Dalkin shook his head. "Constipation still a problem at the Bureau–butt-lipped bowel-heads."

The waitress studied Dalkin. "We no have."

"That's a relief. Give me. . ." he studied a menu. "Lo mein."

"What kind lo mein?"

"I don't know. Chicken, vegetable. Both."

"Mix lo mein?" said the waitress.

"Whatever."

The waitress scribbled, shot Dalkin a puzzled glance and scrammed.

"So, this Willard Stukey character," said Dalkin. "What's the story on him?"

"We're piecing it together. A real head case, this guy. At first we thought he was a terrorist. We were *hoping* that."

"Hoping?" Dalkin cocked his head.

"Sure. This sort of thing's even scarier when you see one determined nutcase pull it off, by himself, without other conspirators for logistical support. We can usually apprehend terrorists before an act because there's always a ring of them, and they take time to plan. But one lone nut who takes his own counsel?" Cloverland shook his head.

"Are you close to catching him?"

"Any minute." Cloverland winked.

"C'mon, Jim–this is me, not some schmuck from the media–turd-eating twats. Lo mein."

"Between you and me," Cloverland leaned forward. "This Stukey nutcase could be anywhere. He rented a car in Jacksonville, Florida, before the attack. It hasn't turned up yet. We got a search warrant for his apartment in New York. Biggest fucking mess you've ever seen. Wet paint everywhere. Now our agents are trying to claim for ruined suits. We've staked it out, but, you heard him on CNN. He's not going back there. From the sound of it, he *may* be headed back to the scene of the crime."

"Oh?"

"You heard it, didn't you? He says he's going after Donald Duck next. We have our psychiatrists on it. The profilers. They say he *will* strike again. They say he loves attention."

"What about his demands? What if–?"

"Don't even think about it," said Cloverland. "You know we can't give into demands. Not with terrorists, not with nuts. It would be like rewarding him. No, we just have to keep our eyes open. And wait for Mr. Stukey to make a mistake."

"You mean strike again."

"He'll fuck up eventually." Cloverland evaded the question. "They always do."

Dalkin reached into his inside blazer pocket and pulled out a video cartridge. "This is a video of the murder," he said. "Once you get him, this is all you'll need to show a jury–jughead judges jerking off."

Cloverland took a swig of beer in faux nonchalance. "We assume this stuff is out there. Every other person at

Disney World has a video camera. But nobody's stepping forward. We don't pay like TV."

"We expect to corner the market on this stuff."

"Oh?"

"You'll see." Dalkin smirked. "In any case, this is all you need. A gift."

"A gift?"

"In return for keeping me promptly updated on every new development. Deal?"

"You and me, working together, Jeff. Just like old times. I get to improve my slang hanging around you. Does this mean a big security job at Disney World when I get forced into retirement?"

"I think Michael Ei-yi-yi-yi . . . Michael Ei-yi . . . oh, fuck it. He's just learned the value of good security."

As hot Hunan-style shredded beef with spicy sauce, mixed lo mein, and a bowl of steamed rice arrived, Cloverland's pager beeped.

The FBI assistant director plucked a Nokia cell phone from his pocket. "What's up?" He listened. "Thanks." He snapped the phone shut. "We just had a break," he said. "They found Stukey's rental car."

12

WILLARD STUKEY YAWNED, stretched, and stepped off the bus in Harrisburg, Pennsylvania. Inside the depot, he consulted a departure schedule. First bus out was an overnight to Chicago. Stukey bought a one-way ticket, cash, and stopped for a draft beer at the small, drab station bar before boarding.

13

HUGH SCRUPULA PERSONALLY accompanied a CNN news crew to visit with Michael Eisner at Disney's Yacht Club Resort.

Jeff Dalkin, back from Washington, greeted them at the door of the Admiral's Suite. It was 8:45 a.m. CNN had been trumpeting a live, exclusive interview with Eisner at ten o'clock.

The Disney chairman was tense when he appeared from a bedroom. Scrupula attempted to engage him in small talk, but Eisner did not even part his tight lips. He glanced around, unsmiling, checking his watch, tapping his right foot.

At five minutes to ten, Eisner quietly sat upon a wing chair next to that of his interviewer, facing a TV camera. He waved off a make-up artist.

Hugh Scrupula, on the phone with CNN's broadcast center in Atlanta, counted down with his fingers from behind the camera. Five-four-three-two-one . . . and they were live.

Said the correspondent: "I'm sitting here in Orlando, Florida, with Disney chairman Michael Eisner. . . ."

Waiting for two eggs, over-easy, a side of bacon, hash-browns, and rye toast in a Chicago Greyhound bus station coffee shop, Willard Stukey's ears perked at the mention of Michael Eisner on a TV set mounted in the corner.

The artist stood, his suit rumpled from doubling as pyjamas, and drew nearer.

"Mr. Eisner," said CNN's correspondent. "This is your first word to the public since Mickey and Minnie Mouse, and forty visitors to Disney World, were murdered by a mad gunman three days ago. How do you feel?"

Eisner shot an irritated look at his interviewer. How did he feel? How the fuck did CNN—and the rest of the world—*think* he felt?

"First of all, Mickey and Minnie Mouse were not murdered," said Eisner. "Employees of the Walt Disney Company, professional actors dressed as Mickey and Minnie, were murdered. Our heartfelt condolences go out to the families of those individuals, and to the families of *everyone* victimized by this senseless act of cowardice."

Senseless? Stukey began to steam. Cowardice? Did this filthy rich jerk not understand that it took tremendous *courage* to stage a live art exhibition at the risk of death or life imprisonment? What did *Eisner* know about art anyway? He was a businessman—guilty of commercializing art in the crassest way imaginable for maximum sponduliks. *Walt* was the true genius. Oh, yeah.

"What are you doing to. . . ?" started the correspondent.

"There's something I want to say," Eisner cut off his interrogator mid-question and faced the camera earnestly. "The Walt Disney Company is offering a one million dollar reward for information leading to the capture of Willard Stukey."

Stukey squirmed amongst others who had grouped to watch the interview on TV.

"Furthermore," Eisner continued. "We are also offering one hundred thousand dollars for video-taped recordings of that madman's attack on our Magic Kingdom Park."

"Why are you...?" asked the interviewer.

Stukey did not stick around for the rest of the question. He stalked off.

"Sir—your breakfast." A waitress pointed to a plate of eggs, bacon, hashbrowns, and rye toast where Stukey had been sitting.

The artist pulled a bankroll from his pocket and plunked a ten dollar bill onto the table. "Keep the change, ma'am. Where's a public phone in this place?"

Hugh Scrupula, still maintaining an open connection to CNN's broadcast center as the Eisner interview continued, could scarcely believe his ears: Willard Stukey was on a CNN line, asking for him.

"Patch him through," snapped Scrupula, trying his best to whisper. "And stay on the line, listen in."

The phone clicked.

"Is that you, Hugh?" asked Stukey's familiar voice.

"Yes, Willard." Scrupula whispered. "It's me."

"I want to talk to Michael Eisner."

"I can't, he's live, what... where are you?"

"Put me on TV with Eisner," demanded Stukey.

Scrupula's mind raced. "Let me think about how to do this."

"I don't have time for thinking," snarled Stukey. "Just put me on with him. Or I'm history. And trust me, I've got more history to make."

"Okay, be patient," said Scrupula. "Control, are you there?"

"Roger," said a third party on the line.

"Can you put Willard on as a voice-over?" asked Scrupula.

"Sure."

"Do it. Alert the correspondent interviewing Eisner. Willard?"

"Still here."

"Hold on," Scrupula directed. "In a few seconds you'll start to hear the broadcast. Wait for your cue."

"Got it," said Stukey. "But hurry, guy. I don't got all day."

The correspondent's face registered astonishment when he learned through his earpiece that Willard Stukey was standing by. He was so taken off guard, he absently neglected to let Michael Eisner finish his sentence.

"I'm told that Willard Stukey, the artist being hunted for the murder of Mickey Mouse, is with us."

Eisner stiffened.

"Willard?" said the correspondent. "Are you there?"

"I'm here." Stukey's voice was heard by those inside Eisner's suite through a TV monitor. And by millions of viewers in the United States and around the world.

"You've been listening to our interview with Disney chairman Michael Eisner?" the correspondent asked deferentially.

"Yup, sure have."

Once he had gotten over the initial shock of Stukey's vocal presence, Eisner considered removing himself from the set. But he thought better of it, deciding to remain cool and unfettered by this strange twist.

"That reward he's offering," said Stukey. "If I turn myself in, could I claim the one million?"

The correspondent looked to the Disney chairman for a response. "Mr. Eisner?"

Eisner bristled. CNN was giving this murderer license to make a mockery of him. "Of course not!"

"How 'bout if I cut you a deal?" said Stukey. "I turn myself in, you give me *half* a million–for my legal expenses–and I *save* you the other half of the reward?"

Eisner folded his arms. "I find your remarks extremely offensive and undeserving of a response."

"That's fine by me," said Stukey. "I don't want your goddamn money anyway. I want my paintings to have a fair showing. I want an exhibition at MoMA *without* help from the corrupt scumbags who manipulate the art world."

"You're dreaming," huffed Eisner.

"Dreaming? *I'm* dreaming? You're one to talk about dreaming, Mr. Eisner. Your whole empire is based on dreams. You make billions of dollars from the dream business. At least my dream isn't based on commerce."

"You're sick!" snapped Eisner. "You've murdered over forty people in cold blood!"

"It was live art," said Stukey. "People are born, they die. Only art prevails. They'll understand me better in a hundred years. That's how long it sometimes takes to understand a great artist."

"I've had enough." Eisner started to rise. "He's nuts. I

refuse to debate this lunatic."

"Before you go, Mr. Eisner," said Stukey, "I want you to know that buying all the videotape of my live art exhibition won't work. When I gun down Donald Duck, I'm gonna videotape it myself for worldwide distribution."

"You sonofabitch!" hollered Eisner. Standing, he turned on the correspondent. "How dare you give this failed artist a platform to say he's going to murder more people!"

The shaken correspondent did not reply.

Nor did Willard Stukey.

"Willard? Willard?" called the correspondent. "Are you still with us?"

Silence.

Then: "I am *not* a failed artist, goddammit!" Stukey was hollering. "What does that idiot know about art anyway? Animated cartoons? Ha! He hasn't seen my paintings. And I don't care if he ever does. But he *is* going to see me kill Donald Duck!"

"He *can't* kill Donald Duck!" screamed an outraged Eisner. "It is impossible to kill a cartoon character! Mickey Mouse is still alive! Mickey Mouse will *always* be alive!"

"Willard?" asked the correspondent. "Willard?"

But Stukey was gone.

Disgusted, Eisner yanked the microphone over his head and flung it across the room. "Interview's over." He was trembling with rage, eyes popping. "Get out, you sons-of-bitches! Get the hell out of my suite! Get the hell out of Disney World!"

The Disney chairman's tantrum was broadcast live. Until Eisner bent down and pulled the plug. CNN went black.

"You!" he pointed at Jeff Dalkin. "Come with me!"

Eisner stormed into another room and slammed the door.

Hugh Scrupula beamed. "That went well," he said to Dalkin.

"You think so?" Dalkin wasn't sure if this was sarcasm or bliss.

"The true test," said Scrupula, "will be how many times they replay it through the day." He smiled broadly. "My guess is every half-hour."

Dalkin shook his head. "That was tenser than a whore on the cathedral steps. Don't you think letting that guy Stukey on the air is promoting him?"

"Promoting him?"

"Worse," said Dalkin. "Egging him on?"

"On one level, yes." Scrupula was solemn now. This was the kind of ethical stuff that media bigwigs occasionally spewed over during lofty meetings back at headquarters. "On another level, it rivets the whole nation onto this manhunt, which causes the FBI and police to focus on this guy until they catch him–like what happened to Andrew Cunanan, the guy who shot Gianni Versace. Remember? Nobody in the media followed Cunanan's killing spree across the U.S. until he gunned down Versace outside his Palm Beach house and it became a major news story."

"Does anyone at your organization alert the Bureau–butt-faced bargsters–when Stukey is on the phone, so they can try to trace him? Lo mein."

Scrupula shook his head. "There isn't time." It sounded lame. "It's not our job," he added.

"What about civic responsibility?"

Michael Eisner popped his head out the door. "Are you coming?"

Dalkin winked. "Be right there, boss—nazi schwinehund, blow me— shit! I didn't mean. . . ."

Eisner slammed the door.

"That was a dumb idea." Eisner fumed. He sat on the corner of a king-size bed. "Ted Turner's going to hear about this. Heads will roll at CNN. Did you know they were going to put that, that murderer on with me?"

"Of course not," said Dalkin. "I don't think anybody knew."

Eisner shook his head, disgusted. "When is the FBI going to catch this guy? It's not like they don't know what he looks like."

"He's probably changed his appearance," said Dalkin. "He's using cash, not credit cards. He abandoned the car he was renting. So if he's traveling, he's using trains or buses."

"Where?" snapped Eisner.

"Where what?"

"Where did they find his car?"

"Reading, Pennsylvania. It was parked at a place called the Peanut Bar."

"Pennsylvania? What . . .?"

Dalkin shrugged. "He's from Kentucky originally. The Bureau—bollocking splatheads—they think he might be heading for his hometown. These guys sometimes do that. One last look. You don't have any Donald Ducks in Kentucky, do you? Lo mein."

Eisner looked at Dalkin like he was nuts. "I know what we'll do," he said. "Double the reward! Make it two million dollars!"

"Why don't you just accept Stukey's offer of a half-million to turn himself in. It's not like you'd really have to pay up."

"No, but the media would slaughter me anyway for agreeing to it. Bad PR. Families of the deceased would form a class-action suit and double whatever they're planning to claim. And get it, too. Attendance at my theme parks is already down thirty percent."

"Okay, we know this Stukey guy wants to murder Donald Duck," said Dalkin.

"He *can't* murder Donald Duck," hissed Eisner.

"No. But he *thinks* he can," said Dalkin. "That's what he's planning. Blatantly. If we're going to catch him, it's because he's coming to us—to Donald Duck. Where is Donald Duck?"

Eisner wrung his hands. "Normally, we have about seven Donald Ducks at Walt Disney World, three at Disneyland in Anaheim, California, and one on our cruise ship. But I just had a call from my operations manager saying our actors are refusing to wear Donald Duck costumes, not even for triple overtime."

"Perfect!" said Dalkin. "We'll put FBI— fart-catching farmyard floggers—into Donald Duck suits!"

Eisner nodded. "How many midgets does the FBI employ?"

"Midgets?" Dalkin squinted.

"That's right," said Eisner. "The actors who do Mickey and Minnie are under five-feet. Midgets."

"Hmmm." Dalkin considered this. "I don't think they even allow midgets into the Bureau—butt-sucking barnyard-bollocking by-the-book bottom-snorters—whew!"

"What about his demand?" said Eisner.

"An exhibition at the New York Museum of Modern Art?"

Eisner nodded.

"The F...F...– fornicating flatfoots–FBI, whew!–they say no."

"The hell with them!" roared Eisner. "It's not their outfit getting shot up. All we need is a broom closet at that museum, hang a few paintings."

"Stukey also wants a review in the *New York Times*. A full page."

"So? The *Times* was willing to print the Unabomber's tract. Let's get them to do a review of this lunatic's art. It's not like people don't know it's a forced thing. Go see them."

"Go see who?"

"Go see the Museum of Modern Art," said Eisner. "And the *New York Times*."

Dalkin nodded. "Can I take the...?"

"No! I'm flying the Gulfstream back to LA at noon."

14

Willard Stukey studied the departure board inside Chicago's Greyhound bus station. He had already decided not to take the first bus out this trip. He knew *exactly* where he wanted to go.

15

Jeff Dalkin trudged down the aisle of a Continental jet at Newark International Airport.

"Thanks for flying with us, Mr. Willis," said a giggly female flight attendant.

"Lo mein," said Dalkin.

"Look! Bruce Willis!" This was a young man standing near a baggage carousel. "He's come home to Jersey!"

Dalkin cursed under his breath. Looking like Bruce Willis was the perfect cover for what he really did. But, hey, it was also a royal pain in the bazongas. How could the real Bruce Willis stand it?

"Manhattan," Dalkin instructed a cab driver. "Corner of Fifth and Fifty-third."

"You got it, Mr. Willis!" The cabbie hit his gas pedal and screeched out of the taxi rank with this prize customer.

That was another thing: every cabbie wanted to race, like he assumed Bruce was in a chase scene.

"So, who youz seeing these days?" asked the cabbie, staring at Dalkin in his rearview mirror.

"I'm getting into a harem thing," Dalkin squawked out the side of his mouth. "Liv Tyler, Sporty Spice, Cameron Diaz—man, she's hot, gives good head. I been working on getting Helen Hunt in the sack. Now there's a hot bitch. Gotta do that before I reconcile with Demi. Lo mein."

"You're gonna get back with Demi?"

"Yeah. The bitch has a three-week period and looks like shit in the morning, but she *is* the mother of my kids, so what the hell."

The cabbie was speechless; just the way Dalkin wanted him. Until they reached Madison Avenue.

"So, you and Demi have patched things up?" The cabbie tried to sound natural.

Dalkin had run into this type many times before. Tabloid tipsters. They were everywhere. Not just cab drivers. Hospital clerks. Fashion boutique salespeople. The hotel concierge.

"Yeah," said Dalkin. "We're sick of lawyers—lying labonzas—trying to leech our money. She's balling Skeet Ulrich, but what the hell—a little practice on someone else can't hurt, maybe even improve her technique. Let me tell ya, fake boobs has got nothin' to do with technique. Lo mein."

The cabbie double parked on Fifty-fourth Street. As cars honked, he furiously pounded digits on a public phone.

"Mr. Duffy? It's me, Joe . . . yeah, I had Bruce Willis in the cab five minutes ago. This is hot, real hot. He's getting back together with Demi! Yeah, but first he wants to do Helen Hunt . . . uh-huh, that's exactly what he said, get her in the sack. And get this, he says Demi's screwing Skeet Ulrich.

Oh, and he kept saying 'lo mein' . . . yeah, lo mein–must be the new Hollywood lingo. What? Of course it was him! Youz think I don't know what Bruce Willis looks like? Youz gonna have to pay me a bonus for this one, Mr. Duffy."

"Where does the curator of this joint hang out?" Dalkin asked a uniformed guard outside the concrete and glass Museum of Modern Art at Eleven West Fifty-third Street.

"There's an office to the right." The guard pointed through a revolving door. "Ask in there."

Dalkin entered, found an office door, slightly ajar. He knocked, pushed it open. "I'd like to see the curator," he announced. "Lo mein."

Two secretaries manning desks dropped their jaws in unison, faces agog. One froze; the other jumped to action, picking up the phone, yakking away.

"He'll be with you in a few minutes, Mr. Willis," said the animated one. "Um, may I have your autograph?"

"Me, too," the other secretary unfroze.

Dalkin shrugged and smirked, and signed Bruce Willis.

Then he sat and read the *New York Times* as the pair tittered and surreptitiously telephoned their relatives.

Soon, the curator entered. In his charcoal gray, double-breasted Hickey-Freeman suit and gray speckled hair and beard, he cut a dashing form, punctuated by a bright red silk hankie that drooped deliberately from his suitcoat pocket.

"Over there," a receptionist pointed officiously.

"I can see, thank you." The curator approached Dalkin. "Mr. Willis?"

Dalkin rose, offered his hand.

"I'm Nathaniel Sugarman, Curator of MoMA. What can I do for you?" His words smelled of pomposity.

"Mr. Curator," Dalkin whispered. "What say we have a word in private?" He motioned his head at the two secretaries, both craning their necks to capture every nuance of the action.

"I have only a few minutes," said Sugarman.

"That's all I need."

"This way." Sugarman led Dalkin to his office, its walls lined with magnificent works by German post-expressionists. "Please, have a seat." He gestured to a stiff wing chair facing his desk.

Dalkin sat.

Sugarman seated himself behind his large desk. He looked Dalkin in the eye. "Wait, don't tell me," he said. "Let me see if I can guess."

Dalkin discerned a bemused twinkle in Sugarman's beady eyes.

"You've taken up painting?" posed Sugarman. He shook his rosy, apple cheeks and smiled what seemed to Dalkin an artificial smile. "You movie stars. You think just because you can act in films, you are natural, multi-talented artists. And you have more money than you know what to do with, so you hire the best art teachers in the world for private lessons. They tell you what to paint, how to paint, what colors to use . . . an advanced form of painting by numbers. The art gallery chains–those you find in shopping malls– print these contrived pieces, number them, and sell them for astronomical prices. And then these faux artists have the audacity to come here and ask for an exhibition of their work. Hmmm, Mr. Willis?"

Dalkin grinned. "That's not why I'm here."

Sugarman looked to heaven. "Praise the Lord."

"Michael Ei-Ei... Ei-yi-yi-yi," Dalkin sang like a Mexican mariachi. "Uh, Michael Ei-Ei–fuck it! You know, the guy who runs Disney?"

"Michael Eisner?"

"That's him! He sent me," said Dalkin. "You heard about how a madman opened fire on people in Disney World earlier this week?"

"It would be very difficult *not* to hear about that," said Sugarman. "It cannot be avoided on television."

"Yeah, well, did you happen to hear that the madman—an artist named Willard Stukey—says he's going to keep popping Disney characters unless his work gets exhibited here, in your museum?"

"That caught our attention briefly." Sugarman paused. "Don't tell me you've come here to suggest that we actually do this?"

Dalkin nodded. "Yep. That's why I'm here."

"It is an outlandish proposition," snapped Sugarman. "You could not possibly expect me to compromise the intregity of my museum in this manner."

"It will save lives," said Dalkin. "Isn't that a consideration?"

"Is it lives you wish to save, Mr. Willis—or is the image of Disney World as a safe family playground at risk? Or are you planning to make a movie about this? Hmmm?"

"I'd expect that kind of cynicism from a cop," said Dalkin. "Not a curator. Lo mein."

"This is New York City," explained Sugarman.

"There are no plans for a movie," said Dalkin. "And

I'm not Bruce W-W-Willis. My name's Jeff Dalkin." Sugarman folded his arms, displaying a pair of antique intaglio cufflinks, and smiled. "Who are you trying to fool?"

"No one. People fool themselves."

"You're *not* Bruce Willis?" Sugarman rubbed his eyes and took a closer look.

"No, I'm Jeff Dalkin. I do special jobs for special clients—dumb mutherfucks. You see, I couldn't control my cursing just now. Bruce W-W-Willis doesn't have Tourette's. I do."

"You have Tourette's?" Sugarman lit up. "It's a fascinating disorder. I've only ever seen it once or twice on television. How long have you been afflicted?"

"Since I was a kid. I used to tell my grade school teachers—nazi schwinehunds—to shove dildos in various body orifices. Odd thing was, I didn't know what a dildo was. It took a psychiatrist—pecksniffing pantload—to tell everyone I couldn't help myself. I told him to fuck off, too. Certain words set it off. Lo mein. Now I keep saying 'lo mein' because I picked it up at a Chinese—midget mutherfucks—restaurant, and it just pops out my mouth."

Sugarman was riveted.

"Now, Mr. Curator," said Dalkin. "We really must do something to stop this Stukey guy—scrotum-faced skag-shooting son-of-a-shag-assed skank!" This last bout wasn't really Tourette's; Dalkin added it for Sugarman's benefit since it seemed to tickle the erudite curator.

"I don't know about this." Sugarman shook his head. "This is *MoMA*." He said MoMA as if it were the Lord Himself.

"Look, everyone will know you're doing it because you

have to stop more people getting killed. It's a noble thing, really. You'll be applauded."

"Let me see the paintings," said Sugarman.

"Does it really matter what they look like?"

"Maybe, maybe not," said Sugarman. "But I think I should see exactly what would be exhibited. In the interim, it will allow time for pause, to consider this proposition." He paused. "Do you still see a psychiatrist for Tourette's?"

"No point," replied Dalkin. "It's incurable. Lo mein."

16

"Hugh?"

"Yes, Willard." CNN's Breaking News producer spoke apprehensively into his telephone.

"I'm here, Hugh."

"Where, Willard? Where are you?"

"Put me on the air and I'll tell you," said Stukey.

"I don't know if I can do that, Willard. We've taken a lot of heat for...."

"Put me on or I'm hanging up."

"Um...."

"I mean it, Hugh."

"Okay. Hold on." Scrupula connected to broadcast control. "I have Willard Stukey on line. Can we put him on?"

"Your call, Hugh," said the broadcast director. "We can do it, technically speaking, but you take responsibility."

"Do it." Scrupula re-connected to Stukey. "Okay, Willard. Listen for your cue."

Through the receiver, Stukey heard an anchor interrupt the afternoon yak-a-thon and announce that Willard

63

Stukey was on the phone. "Are you there, Mr. Stukey?" asked the anchor.

"Yeah, guy," Stukey replied. "I'm here."

"Uh, can you tell us where you are?"

"Sure. I'm outside a Disney merchandise shop." Stukey paused. "I'm going to teach Michael Eisner never, ever to refer to me as a failed artist."

"What are you planning?"

"I'm going to shoot the place up. Kill as many customers and sales staff as I can."

The anchor gasped. "Where exactly are you?"

"You want to break some news?" said Stukey. He spoke slowly. "Okay, you be the first. I like CNN. I'm in Manhattan. At the fives."

"The fives?"

"Yup. Better call an ambulance. No. Better call twenty."

"Mr. Stukey, don't. . . ."

"See ya–bye." Stukey let the receiver dangle, unhooked, then turned from the public phone kiosk and marched into Disney's flagship emporium on the corner of Fifth Avenue and Fifty-fifth Street.

The artist did not search for inspiration this rampage; he had no time to luxuriate in live art. Having alerted the country to his whereabouts–if they believed him–he'd get right to the point: the point of his Hechler & Koch MPSKA4 9mm machine pistol.

Stukey strode to the center of the shop, at the base of the up escalator, whipped out his weapon and whirled 360 degrees, firing rounds.

Shoppers fell; blood was shed by the pint. Moans, gasps, death throes. And all the while, a Donald Duck cartoon played on twelve screens combined into one.

This irony was lost on Stukey as he retraced his steps to the front entrance. He turned and gave the shambles of his creation one final spray of hot lead. Then he tucked the weapon beneath his jacket, cut around the corner onto Fifty-fifth Street, and jumped into a taxi on Madison Avenue.

Had it not been for Stukey's pre-emptive call to CNN, the police might have thought this was a copy-cat crime, as eyewitnesses reported the killer to be clean shaven, wearing a suit and tie.

Jeff Dalkin covered his ears as he exited the Museum of Modern Art. Before him, a convoy of ambulances congested Fifth Avenue, lights flashing, sirens ululating; the decibel count all combined was excruciating. Dalkin could not hear the whistling of his cell phone.

The lightweight StarTac rang again as Dalkin reached Avenue of the Americas, where he planned to hail a cab and escape the commotion.

He flipped it open. "Yeah-what?"

"HAVE YOU HEARD WHAT JUST HAPPENED?"

"Who is this?"

The circuit inside the receiver fuzzied at such a high vocal volume.

"IT'S ME!"

"Mr. Ei-yi-yi. . . ?"

"YES, GODDAMMIT! YOU HAVEN'T HEARD?"

"Heard what?"

"THAT MANIAC! THAT MURDERING BASTARD! HE JUST SHOT A BUNCH OF PEOPLE AT OUR STORE IN NEW YORK CITY!"

"Where's the store?"

"FIFTH AVENUE AND FIFTY-FIFTH STREET!"

"Jesus Christ, that's three blocks away. I'm on my way. Stay calm."

"STAY CALM? ARE YOU OUT OF YOUR MIND?"

"I'm going to the scene. Where are you?"

"ON THE JET!"

Dalkin snapped his phone shut, whipped around and jogged up Fifty-third Street. He was confronted by pandemonium, carnage—and a police roadblock. A good chunk of Fifth Avenue was closed off, chock-ablock-with ambulances. Multiple gurneys were being rolled into Disney's merchandise mart; paramedics ran in circles.

"No one gets through!" barked a police officer.

"I work for Michael Ei-yi-yi—rich little ratfuck—*Eisner!* Whew! I have to get through!"

The officer stepped back, mostly in awe. "Go see that guy!" He pointed to a plainclothes detective surveying the manic scene.

Dalkin strode over.

The detective looked up and smiled. "Bruce Willis? What are *you* doing here?" He offered his hand. "Good to meet ya."

Dalkin shook the detective's hand. "I'm Jeff Dalkin, not Bruce W-W-Willis. I work for Disney. What happened here?"

The detective gestured at the commotion. "The Mickey murderer struck again. He shot up a shop this time. I got seven confirmed dead and a whole bunch wounded. Hank Rookstool, Homicide." The detective took off his sunglasses and squinted at Dalkin. "Are you sure you're not Bruce Willis?"

"Did they catch him?" asked Dalkin.

"Stukey? Nah. He melted away. The feds are on their way. He's made their Top Ten list. I can't let you get any closer, our men are picking up empty cartridges. Damn, if you ain't Bruce Willis, you must be his twin brother."

Dalkin's phone whistled. He flipped it open. "Yeah–what?"

"What's going on?" snapped Eisner.

"At least seven dead. Many wounded. No sign of Stukey."

Dalkin held the receiver six inches from his ear as Eisner unleashed a torrent of obscenities.

"Is that Michael Eisner?" Detective Rookstool whispered.

"Yeah," said Dalkin. "He's got Tourette's."

Willard Stukey climbed out of a taxi in front of Penn Station on Seventh Avenue. First train out was a Shore Points commuter to Bay Head. The artist paid cash for a ticket at NJ Transit and boarded.

One hour later, Stukey disembarked at Red Bank, New Jersey, beckoned by its small-town proportions.

"Any hotels within walking distance?" he asked a ticket clerk inside the small wooden station.

"Molly Pitcher Inn. Four blocks that way." The clerk pointed. "Turn left."

Fifteen minutes later, Stukey was ensconced in a room overlooking the picturesque Navesink River. He tuned a TV set to CNN, which was re-playing his chilly phone chat with an ashen-faced news anchor. Then the action switched live to a reporter on Fifth Avenue in Manhattan.

"We're hearing from police sources on the scene that, for this attack, Willard Stukey was wearing a business suit."

"Uh-oh, here we go again." Stukey rummaged bedside drawers for a Monmouth County telephone directory. He flipped through its yellow pages and found what he wanted.

Two hours later, the famous incognito artist emerged from Garmany on Broad Street, fashionably attired in an Italian tweed sportcoat, corduroy trousers, tassled loafers, and a fedora on his head.

17

Jeff Dalkin was waiting at Teterborough, a small airfield in northern New Jersey, when Michael Eisner's Gulfstream kissed the tarmac and slid to a halt.

Eisner stepped off the jet and darted into a big black Disney limousine. He glanced at Dalkin, next to him on the back seat, but did not say a word, staring straight ahead, his system one notch below clinical shock.

Then Eisner shook his head back and forth. "Why haven't they caught him?" he muttered. "Why haven't they caught him? Why? Why? Why haven't they got him yet?" He looked at Dalkin.

"They need a lucky break." Dalkin shrugged. "No lucky breaks yet. Lo mein."

Eisner's face reddened. His mouth erupted to say something, but clenched before any words could escape, creating a vacuum-like gasp. He waited a good ten seconds. Then, in a deliberate, controlled tone, he issued his command: "I want you to fly to Washington to find out. . ." then he lost control ". . . find out what those mutherfuckers at the FBI

are doing to catch this goddamn maniac!"
"Lo mein," said Dalkin.
"And quit saying lo mein!"
Dalkin nodded. "Can I take the Gulf . . . ?"
"No!"

18

WILLARD STUKEY PERCHED himself upon a stool at the International Bar of the Molly Pitcher Inn to watch CNN's Special Report about his own life: a patchwork quilt of interviews with friends Stukey hadn't seen in ten to twenty years. He sipped his favorite libation, Pernod and water, and sighed contentedly.

19

JEFF DALKIN POPPED his head forward, into the cabin of a Delta Shuttle aircraft. "What kind of jet is this?" he asked.

"Seven-thirty-seven," chirped the bubbly flight attendant.

"But these things are still falling out of the sky. A bum rudder." Dalkin made a diving-motion with his hand. "Kaboom!"

"You could try US Airways," huffed the flight attendant

"Yeah, right. *They* wanted to stick me on a DC-nine, for chrissakes. Never mind. Lo mein." Dalkin pushed forward and found himself an aisle seat by an emergency door.

20

"JEFF DALKIN?" A fat, African-American black woman-of-color confronted Dalkin face-to-face after inspecting his driver's license. "Yo' look like Bruce Willis to me."

She said this, not in deference to the great actor, but in defiance, as she thought she was being conned. And it was her job, as guardian of the hideously ugly J. Edgar Hoover Building, not to be conned. Not even by Bruce Willis.

"I'm working undercover," whispered Dalkin. "Could you kind of keep it down?"

"Then what you doin' here?" she demanded.

"Just call R. James Cloverland, like I asked, and find out," said Dalkin.

Other persons waiting inside the Badge Room for Bureau appointments tittered as the man who resembled Bruce Willis took a pew.

"Mr. Dalkin, if that's who you be," called the African-American black woman-of-color. "Somebody coming down for you now."

Dalkin felt a Tourettic outburst surging through his body. It wasn't a word or a phrase triggering it this time; it was his former employer's headquarters. He stood and shook his head wildly, in a vain effort to stave it off.

"Big black bazoomas bouncing over my bazooka!" he blurted.

The Badge Room froze into silence.

"Huh?" This was Dalkin. "What? Oh, no! Shit! Bargs! Lo mein!" Dalkin opened the glass door and stepped out.

Twenty seconds later a uniformed security guard approached him. "What's the problem, mister?" He looked closer. "Bruce Willis?"

"I'm waiting to see James Cloverland," said Dalkin. "Assistant Director of the FB—bad-assed butt-fucks—I!"

"Yeah, sure, Bruce. Whatever." The guard backed away. "Take it easy, man. I'm cool."

R. James Cloverland's secretary approached. "Mr. Dalkin?"

"Yeah. Get me outta here."

Dalkin followed the secretary across a cobblestoned courtyard, through a security post and a couple of turnstiles.

It was while passing a life-size portrait of William Webster, in an oddly shaped foyer, that Dalkin lost it again.

"Willie Webster whacks his wang in the whizzer! Oh, shit! Sorry, I. . . ."

"It's okay," the secretary grinned. "Mr. Cloverland warned me."

They stepped into a crowded elevator and ascended.

"Lo mein," said Dalkin. "Lo mein lo mein lo mein lo mein." This was a tactic Dalkin executed, vaccination-style, to keep his Tourettic urge at bay.

Cloverland was waiting in his sumptuous, spacious seventh floor office. He stood and greeted his old chum with a smile, then turned solemn. "The pressure is on."

"I should fucking well hope so. Michael Ei-yi-yi-yi..." Dalkin sang like a Mexican mariachi. "Shit, fuck, lo mein. My boss—blow a fart—is going bananas."

"We've put Stukey on The List." Cloverland said this with satisfaction, like it was a big deal.

"I don't give a turd about your top ten chart. What leads are you working on?"

"Leads?" Cloverland shrugged. "The sonofabitch has disappeared again."

"How can he just disappear?" Dalkin pitched himself into an easy chair and propped his loafered feet onto the coffee table.

"In New York?" Cloverland rumped his own rear. "You're kidding, right? You know how it works, Jeff. We track people through cars and credit card usage. This guy's not using either. We need a lucky break. He'll make a mistake eventually. And now we've got CNN on our side ..."

"CNN? Turd and maggots." Dalkin made a flog-the-log gesture with his right hand. "They're jerking him on."

"Maybe. But at least they flash his picture constantly. Someone will recognize him. A motel clerk, a bus driver, someone."

"Do you have any clue where he is right now?"

Cloverland shrugged. "Our profilers are making assessments."

"And?"

"They just don't know." Cloverland checked his wristwatch. "He could be anywhere within fifteen hours' ground travel of New York City. We're looking at bus routes, train schedules. He's not sophisticated. We don't think he has false ID, or a plan to flee the country. But he's very creative. His paintings...."

"Ah, that's something else I want to discuss. What about his paintings?"

"We brought them to Quantico for psychoanalysis," said Cloverland. "Our top psychologists examined them."

"And?"

"Like I said, this Stukey is a highly creative individual. They've never seen anything like it."

"Are you finished with them?" asked Dalkin.

"The paintings?"

"Yeah."

"I guess so," Cloverland shrugged.

"Can I borrow a couple?"

Cloverland squinted one eye. "Why would you want to do that?"

"Uh, Michael Ei-yi-yi-yi . . . yi-yi! Shit! Fuck! Lo mein! My boss—nazi schwinehund—wants his own psychologist to look them over."

Cloverland looked Dalkin in the eye. "C'mon, you're not thinking of. . .?"

"So what if we are? My boss—blow a fart—is frustrated. He wants this guy behind bars, where he can't shoot any more people in his stores and theme parks. And if you're telling me your outfit doesn't have a clue where he is, we have to pursue every avenue open to us. Lo mein."

"Including giving in to his demands?" Cloverland's tone hardened.

"If need be," said Dalkin. "Look, we can create the *illusion* that Stukey's work is being exhibited at MoMA, for his benefit only. But to get that going, I need to show MoMA's curator a couple of paintings."

"Why?"

"Because he's Oz. And he demanded the witch's broomstick. Lo mein."

Cloverland shook his head. "I can't do that."

"What do you mean you can't do that? Blow me. Why the hell not? Those paintings aren't material evidence. They're not even your property. They belong to Willard Stukey."

"I can't believe my ears!" Cloverland's eyeballs popped. "You're defending Stukey's property rights now?"

"That's got nothing to do with it."

"Whatever the case," said Cloverland. "Stukey's paintings certainly don't belong to you or Michael Eisner."

"Stukey said he wants them displayed at MoMA. You heard him. Everybody heard him. So, on behalf of MoMA's curator, I am requesting that they be handed over. Do you want us to hire a lawyer–lying labonzas?"

"You wouldn't do that."

"I wouldn't, but Michael Ei-yi-yi-yi . . . yi-yi-yi-yi! Goddammit! My boss–blow a fart–will send a *team* of lawyers–lying labonzas."

Cloverland got up, ambled to his desk and activated his intercom. "Sherry? Call Quantico and tell them to get two of Stukey's paintings over to me ASAP . . . huh? . . . no, any two." He put the phone down and faced Dalkin. "Satisfied?"

21

It was evening in Red Bank, New Jersey, and Willard Stukey was glued to the TV set in his room at the Molly Pitcher Inn. Every hour, the news hounds at CNN presented a new face—someone, anyone it seemed, who knew Stukey at some point of his life, however fleetingly. A boyhood neighbor, a high school sweetheart, and now . . . and now here was Mr. Floto. He looked older, as he should. Stukey was mesmerized by his image. He had a bad feeling about what was to come.

"You were Willard Stukey's art teacher in eighth grade," a CNN reporter prodded. "What can you tell us about him?"

"He was a mediocre student," said Mr. Floto, smiling. Gloating, it seemed to Stukey. "He never listened. Did his own thing."

"Isn't that what artists are supposed to do, goddammit?" Stukey erupted. "This is *my* moment, not *yours*, you dumb sonofabitch!"

Floto continued: "Willard showed no promise whatsoever as an artist. I'm surprised he calls himself one."

Stukey threw a tasseled loafer at the TV. What did Mr. Floto know about art anyway? With his obsession for colored tiles—hardly a qualification for being an art teacher, even by elementary school standards. Mr. Floto had handed out colored titles and ordered his students to arrange them in collage to his requirements. Nazi-style art. Soviet-era art. And now this so-called teacher had the gall to malign a true artist on national television!

"Hugh?" Stukey whispered, then paused. "It's me."

"Willard?" Hugh Scrupula's tone was taut. "Where are you?"

"Ha!"

"You've got to give yourself up," Scrupula scolded.

"I want to, Hugh. I really do." Stukey spoke earnestly. "And that's just what I plan to do. After my exhibition at MoMA."

"I can't put you on the air."

"You kidding, Hugh? I'm all that's *on* the air. I'm irritated about something. I want to make a statement, that's all."

"Okay, I'll write it down. Shoot." Scrupula paused. "Sorry, wrong choice of words."

"No, Hugh. You feel the artistry, too. It's at play around us. Here it is, Hugh, my statement: Mr. Floto has his head up his colon. Rather than allow his art students to flourish, he tried to quash every creative impulse they had. He is an *anti-*artist. For this, the sentence is death. I will sacrifice him to Catherine of Bologna."

"Who?"

"C'mon, Hugh—you kidding? Everybody knows Catherine of Bologna is the patron saint of art. I'd sue Mr. Floto for libel, but it takes too much time and money. Better just to snuff the bastard. And I'm getting better at it, Hugh. My bus is boarding. See ya–bye."

Stukey hooked the receiver onto its cradle at Red Bank station and, fedora tipped over his brow, boarded a train.

22

JEFF DALKIN'S CELL PHONE whistled as he made his way through the Marine Terminal at New York's LaGuardia Airport. He set down a large package and fumbled for his phone. "Yeah-what?"

"We've had a break," said James Cloverland. "You're on your cell phone? I'll be cryptic. The guy we're hunting is in New Jersey."

"How do you know?"

"We finally got CNN to watch for his call on Caller ID. He called them thirty minutes ago from a pay phone in Red Bank, near the Jersey shore. He was about to board a bus."

"To where?"

"We don't exactly know. But we have an idea where he's headed. I can't say any more over the phone."

"Okay," said Dalkin. "I'll get back to DC this evening. Lo mein." Dalkin flipped the phone shut, picked up his package and aimed himself at the taxi rank.

Without an appointment, Dalkin had to wait an hour-

and-twenty-minutes to see Nathaniel Sugarman of the Museum of Modern Art. And when he was finally ushered into the curator's office, Sugarman was cool and aloof, as if he had hoped Dalkin would never return.

"I got what you asked for," said Dalkin.

Sugarman fluttered his eyelids imperiously. "Oh?"

"A couple of paintings by Willard Stukey. The Mickey murderer. Remember?"

Sugarman was noncommital.

Dalkin parked his package on a chair. "Do you have a scissors?"

Sugarman, still sitting, opened his desk drawer, found a scissors, pushed it reluctantly across his broad desk.

Dalkin cut into the brown paper, unwrapped the canvases and, with both hands, held the first painting up.

The curator looked at it and rose to his feet. He studied it a full thirty seconds, eyes wide, then broke into a smile that caused his apple-red cheeks to swell. "It's magnificent!" he pronounced.

"You're being sarcastic." Dalkin flipped the canvas around to inspect it himself. He saw blobs of color. "Right?"

"Show me the other one," said Sugarman impatiently.

Dalkin dropped the first picture to the floor.

"Careful with that!" Sugarman admonished.

Dalkin held up the second painting.

Sugarman gasped. "Incredible!"

Dalkin flipped it around. More color blobs. "You like them?"

"Like them?" Sugarman bubbled over. "I *adore* them!"

"Okay, joke's over," snapped Dalkin. "You might be the curator of a fancy museum, but I don't have time to dick around . . ."

"Young man," said Sugarman sternly, "I never joke about matters of art. These paintings are magnificent. Abstract expressionism at its most provocative. Modern masterpieces. The man who painted these pictures is an artistic genius. Is this really that, that Mickey murderer?"

Dalkin nodded. "Yep. I got them from the F . . . shit. . . F . . . fuck . . . F . . . flatulating faggots . . . FBI! Whew! They took them directly from Stukey's studio."

"Are there more?" Sugarman clasped his hands.

Dalkin shrugged. "A whole roomful, I think. As far as I know, this guy Stukey has never sold a painting." Dalkin examined the paintings, now propped against the front of Sugarman's desk. "Are they that good?"

"That good? They are magnificent! Do you know what magnificent means? I would hang these pictures in my museum. I would give them a room of their own." Sugarman rubbed his hands gleefully.

"So this means you're willing to stage an exhibition?" asked Dalkin.

"An exhibition? Yes, of course we'll exhibit these pictures." Sugarman paused, in deep thought. "But exhibitions take time."

"How much time?"

"Our calendar is full for the next twelve months."

"No, no, no." Dalkin shook his head. "The purpose of this exercise is to stage an exhibition within a couple days."

"But," Sugarman protested, "this work warrants thought. And planning. We need lead time. It would be a shame to simply hang these paintings in a room and shine lights on them."

Dalkin gritted his teeth. "It'll be a bigger shame if more people get killed by this maniac. You're telling me that because this guy's work is so good, it has to wait?" A new idea struck Dalkin. He picked up the paintings.

"What are you doing?" Sugarman wiped beads of perspiration from his forehead with a linen hankie.

"I'm taking these pictures to another art museum. Maybe Chicago."

"No, No! This is a once-in-a-lifetime find! I must have them."

"Sorry." Dalkin began to re-wrap the paintings.

"But, the artist himself asked that they be exhibited here."

"Consider me his agent," said Dalkin. "I'm making the decisions."

"I can't lose them!" Sugarman wrung his hands around his wrists.

"Consider them lost, buster, unless you put your ass in gear and organize an exhibition by next weekend." Dalkin tied string around the package.

"It's rather hasty." Sugarman hemmed and hawed. "But... yes, we'll do it! How many pictures has he painted."

"I could get maybe twenty," Dalkin guessed.

"How fast can you transport them to me?"

23

As DIRECTED BY R. James Cloverland's secretary, Jeff Dalkin cabbed to Clyde's, Chevy Chase, arriving a few minutes past seven p.m.

The assistant FBI director was waiting in a downstairs booth.

"Mr. Willis?" gasped a pretty young hostess. "Are you here shooting a movie?"

Dalkin smirked. "Lo mein." He looked around and glimpsed Cloverland. "My party's already here," he fended off the fawning, menu-waving hostess and strode off.

She whispered into an intercom, her direct link to the floor above. "Bruce Willis is here. He's making a movie called *Lo Mein!*"

Cloverland was already sipping a tumbler of Myer's rum, slice of lime.

A waiter appeared at Dalkin's side immediately. "A drink, Mr. Willis?"

"Yeah. Lemme have a decent glass of white wine."

"We have Kendall Jackson special vintner's reserve."

"Do it," said Dalkin.

The waiter schooched.

"You really play it up, don't you?" said Cloverland.

"Huh?"

"Your Bruce Willis looks."

"Oh, yeah. That's what they want." Dalkin shrugged. "They don't believe me anyway when I say I'm *not* Bruce W-W-Willis. So, what's the deal on Stukey?"

Cloverland hunched over his libation. "He was in New Jersey this morning. We're luring him to his hometown, in Kentucky."

"How?"

"We realized he was reacting to whatever was said on CNN about him. So we got his old art teacher from grade school in Louisville, an Arthur Floto, to question his ability as an artist." Cloverland winked. "That's what really rattles his cage. Sure enough, he calls CNN immediately and says he's going to pop Floto for bad-mouthing him. So now we've got Floto's house covered. It's just a matter of hours, we think, before this slippery fish comes after our bait."

"You knew about this when I saw you this morning?" said Dalkin.

"Of course, but I wanted to hook our fish before writing the menu."

"Not bad," said Dalkin. "My boss—blow a fart—will be gratified to hear you're not scratching your balls, waiting for a lucky break. Floto, lo mein."

"I'd appreciate your not telling him just yet. This is a sensitive operation."

"You kidding? Ei-Ei . . . yi-yi-yi," Dalkin sang like a Mexican mariachi. "My boss—blow me, shit, fuck, lo mein, Floto. He *wants* this guy caught."

"You know how we feel about the flow of information outside the Bureau. We've done studies on this: for every one person you tell, seven find out."

"Ei–yi-yi-yi-yi-yi! He'll keep his mouth shut. Who do you think he's gonna tell, CNN? Turds and maggots. By the way, I need some more of those paintings."

"Why?"

"MoMA has agreed to an exhibition."

"But we're going to catch this guy," Cloverland protested.

"He's not caught yet."

Cloverland sighed. "It'll send the wrong message to kooks and wackos everywhere."

Dalkin ignored this. "How many paintings do you have?"

"One hundred and twenty-six, not counting the two I gave you this morning."

"I need eighteen more."

Cloverland nodded. "The Bureau does not sanction this."

"Noted, counsellor. Lo mein, Floto."

24

Outside Arthur Floto's modest house in Bardstown, Kentucky, a dozen FBI special agents disguised as gardeners, cable TV repairmen and sewage technicians milled around, watching and waiting in six-hour shifts for Willard Stukey to appear.

Stukey was out there, all right–only much further out than anyone imagined. The artist was absorbing a desert landscape, courtesy of an Amtrak train, and longing for his oil paints. Stukey had never been out to the West Coast. Now he had a good reason to visit.

25

"I'D LIKE TO SEE the arts editor," said Jeff Dalkin.

"Uh, Bruce Willis?" The receptionist of the *New York Times* practically jumped out of her chair. "Of course!" She picked up her phone and yakked that Bruce Willis was in reception for an appointment. She turned to Dalkin. "Uh, he's not expecting you, but he says to let you up, that way, fourth floor." She pointed to an elevator bank.

"What's his name?" Dalkin asked.

"Oh, it's Randall Twining the Third."

Dalkin stepped into an elevator, ascended, got out at the fourth floor.

A nerdy type in wire rim glasses and red suspenders was waiting.

"You Randy?" asked Dalkin.

"Randall Twining." The arts editor put out his hand. "Nice to meet you, Mr. Willis."

"I'm not Bruce W-W-Willis."

Randall Twining chuckled. "No? Then who?"

"Jeff Dalkin."

"I see." Twining winked. Or was it a twitch? "I didn't know

you were a method actor."

"What?"

"You're playing a character named Jeff Dalkin, right?" Twining winked or twitched again. "In a movie called *Lo Mein*?"

"What the hell are you talking about?"

"There was a squib about it in the Style section of today's *Washington Post.* You're making a movie on location in DC. Right?"

"Wrong, Randall. I don't make movies. I work for Michael Ei. . . oh shit . . . Ei . . . oh fuck . . . Ei-yi-yi-yi!" Dalkin sang like a Mexican mariachi who'd swallowed the worm after finishing a bottle of cheap tequila.

Randall Twining blushed, having the peachy, lightly freckled complexion of a man who blushed easily. Or was it rosacea?

"I'm working the Willard Stukey case," said Dalkin.

"You're already making a movie about the Mickey Murder Manhunt?" said an astonished Twining. "They haven't even caught him yet!"

"I'm not Bruce W-W-Willis!" Dalkin clenched his teeth. "I just *look* like him."

"You're *not* Bruce Willis?"

"That's exactly right. I'm not Bruce W-W-Willis. I'm Jeff Dalkin."

Twining pushed his head forward for a closer look. "But you look just like him!"

"I'm not him. Trust me on this, Randy. My name is Jeff Dalkin and I need to talk to you about Willard Stukey."

Twining shrugged. "What about Willard Stukey?"

"MoMA is going to exhibit his paintings."

"Why?"

"Can we go into your office and discuss this?" Dalkin nodded at a gaggle of newsies tittering nearby.

"Of course." Twining led Dalkin to a shoebox with a window; took a seat behind his cluttered desk, shaking his head. "You're really not Bruce Willis?"

"Really not, Randy."

"And you're not his twin brother?"

"Nope."

"Have you ever met him?"

"Bruce? No, but I think I've caused him to sue a number of people."

"I don't understand."

"Tabloid tipsters," said Dalkin. "The snoops are everywhere. Say I'm with a date—it ends up in the *National Enquirer*. Then Bruce W-W-Willis sues them for libel."

"This would make a good story for one of our feature writers," said Twining.

"Not interested." Dalkin shook his head. "I work undercover."

"For Michael Eisner?"

"Uh-huh. How familiar are you with this Mickey Murder Manhunt?"

"Are you joking?" said Twining. "It's impossible *not* to be familiar with it. Every TV newscast, every radio talk show, every newspaper headline...."

"Good, then you know that this guy Stukey says he'll give himself up if his conditions are met."

"Oh, now I get it. You want my paper to publish a review of Stukey's art?" Twining folded his arms.

Dalkin nodded. "That's it, Randy. MoMA's going to

exhibit Stukey's paintings this weekend. Twenty of them. That's condition number one satisfied. Now, if you're willing to print a review, both conditions will be met, he'll give himself up, nobody else gets killed. Floto, lo mein."

"What makes you think he'll really surrender?"

"Motivation," said Dalkin. "He wants to be famous."

"He's already that."

"Exactly. Now he wants his paintings looked at."

"But he's facing the death penalty!"

"He wants to be martyred for his art," said Dalkin. "A van Gogh complex, I don't know."

"Why didn't he just take his paintings around to galleries like everyone else?"

"He tried that. The Bureau—butt-faced back-assed bird-turds—found a bunch of rejection letters."

Twining was riveted by Dalkin's outburst. "Say, do you have Tourette's?"

Dalkin nodded sheepishly.

"I've heard about Tourette's syndrome," said Twining, "but I've never met anyone actually afflicted."

"You actually have now," said Dalkin. "I'm actually afflicted up the wazoo. Lo mein, Floto."

Twining snapped back to business. "Is the FBI in on this?"

"They're actually trying to catch Stukey," said Dalkin.

"I mean, are they part of this plan to meet Stukey's conditions?"

"This is all actually off the record," said Dalkin. "Right?"

"You never said that."

"I'm actually saying it now. This is so fucking off-the-record it's actually pathetic. The Bureau—big-assed pantloads—don't even like this plan. Michael . . . oh shit . . . Michael . . . oh no . . . Ei-yi-yi-yi!" Dalkin sang like a Mexican mariachi, eyes popping and rolling.

"I wondered why you did that before," said Twining. "It's part of Tourette's, right?"

"No shit, Sherlock. You think I do this to entertain people? My boss—blow a fart, nazi schwinehund—wants Stukey behind bars, whatever it takes. The FBI—federal fuck-ups from fart-town—want to *catch* him. It's a macho thing, actually. Lo mein, Floto."

"I can't make this decision on my own," said Twining. "The editor has to agree."

"Once you go up the ladder," said Dalkin, "it gets escalated into a big deal. I don't want to make a big deal out of this. I'm here to let you know that Stukey's paintings will be exhibited at MoMA this weekend. What do you normally do when MoMA stages an exhibition?"

"We review it."

"Exactly! So I'm actually just alerting you that this extra-ordinary exhibition is about to take place. Just do your job, nothing more." Dalkin winked.

"How did you get Nathaniel Sugarman to go along with this?" asked Twining.

"I'm actually glad that actually interests you." Dalkin rose to leave. "I suggest you call Sugarman and ask him directly. Blow me, lo mein, Floto."

26

"WE BRING YOU A major new development in the Mickey Murder Manhunt," Bernard Shaw began CNN's six o'clock newscast. "The Museum of Modern Art in New York City announced a short time ago that they will exhibit the paintings of Willard Stukey this weekend. Stukey is the subject of a national manhunt for murdering over fifty people in two Disney-related attacks."

Willard Stukey, watching while he cleaned his Hechler & Koch MPSKA4 9mm machine pistol, put down the weapon to focus on Bernard Shaw.

"MoMA's curator, Nathaniel Sugarman, announced that he would display Stukey's work on its own merits, and that Stukey's demand for a showing has in no way compromised the museum's integrity, but only accelerated the time frame."

Stukey's jaw dropped. "What the. . . ?"

"But," added Bernard Shaw, "that will satisfy only *one* of Stukey's conditions, delivered live on CNN by the Mickey murderer himself. It is uncertain whether or not his second condition—a full page review in the *New York Times*—will be met. A spokesman for the *New York Times* has told CNN that it will treat Stukey's exhibition as it would any other."

"Ha!" Stukey muttered darkly. He looked out the window of his motel room. In the distance, a faux mountain—the Matterhorn—peaked majestically above Disneyland's Magic Kingdom.

27

JEFF DALKIN SAT inside a Disney stretch limousine reading the *National Enquirer.* Its lead story detailed how Bruce Willis planned to reconcile with Demi Moore after bedding Cameron Diaz and Helen Hunt. "I can't live without Demi's fake boobs," Willis was quoted as having sobbed to an unnamed friend.

Outside the parked limo, a long queue snaked down Fifth Avenue, emanating from the ticket kiosk of the Museum of Modern Art around the corner on Fifty-third Street.

It was nine a.m. Saturday morning, an hour before the museum's doors would open. Television lights illuminated the front entrance.

Randall Twining the Third, arts editor of the *New York Times*, had already viewed the Willard Stukey Exhibition at a press preview the night before. He had walked, poker-faced, from picture to picture, and left quickly without a word.

28

AT SEVEN A.M. West Coast time, Willard Stukey rose and switched on his TV. Reporting live from New York City, CNN announced that MoMA was being mobbed; that the line to get into the Willard Stukey Exhibition was three hours long.

"This isn't happening," Stukey muttered. "Just an illusion. Do they think I'm nuts?" He switched to channel seven. ABC News was broadcasting live from MoMA on Fifty-third Street. He switched to channel two. CBS was doing the same thing. Channel four. Identical. "They're all in on it." Stukey switched off the TV. Enough of this nonsense. He had work to do.

"Where do all the characters hang out?" asked Stukey, looking like a toontown character himself, fedora tipping over his forehead.

"There are always a few on Town Square," said a pimply teenager in a candy-striper shirt and Disney cap. He stopped sweeping Main Street, U.S.A., to point.

"Where can I find a *lot* of them," Stukey pressed. He was nervous and impatient. Disneyland, after all, wasn't exactly the safest place in the world for him to hang out just now. Who knew what security precautions were underway? And where was everyone? The park was sparsely populated and quiet.

"Try Toontown."

"Toontown?"

"Mickey's Toontown. That's where Mickey and all his friends live."

"Used to," sneered Stukey. "Where's that?"

"Through Cinderella's Castle, behind Fantasyland."

"Thanks." Stukey strode the length of Main Street, USA, through the castle, into Fantasyland, a swirl of color and motion.

Color excited Stukey, rejuvenated his spirit. A sign to Mickey's Toontown pointed him onward.

And then he was there: a down-scaled neighborhood of colorful cottages. Mickey's house. And next to that, Donald Duck's abode.

Stukey fingered the machine pistol beneath his jacket and strolled inside; he wandered from room to room.

"Isn't the duck home?" he barked at a pretty hostess.

"The characters are in our Character Hall of Fame," she replied.

Stukey grunted and exited. Perspiration dripped down his face as the California sun beat down upon his tweedy, fedora-capped figure.

Inside the air-conditioned Hall of Fame, two lines to see characters slowed Stukey's pace. And yet another merchandise emporium!

Twenty minutes later, the *Mickey and His Friends* queue led to a room into which Stukey and seven others were shuffled for picture-taking.

Daisy Duck, Goofy, and Snow White cuddled with kids as cameras flashed.

Stukey snuck up to a female steward, whose job it was to shepherd folks in and out. "Psst," he said. "Where's Donald?"

"Donald?"

"Donald Duck," prodded Stukey. "Where's Donald Duck?"

"Donald's not here today." The hostess smiled.

"Not here?"

"Haven't you heard about the Mickey Murder Manhunt?" she whispered.

Stukey shrugged and looked away.

"He threatened to kill Donald Duck," she said sweetly. "So Donald has been keeping a low profile."

Stukey felt an urge to pull out his gun and spray bullets at Daisy and Goofy and Snow White and everyone else, including this Stepford Wife of a hostess. But he repulsed it. Real art had meaning.

"Sir?" The hostess penetrated Stukey's spinning brain. "Would you like your child to pose with Daisy Duck instead?" She looked around. "Which one is yours?"

Stukey stalked out of the chamber, into a corridor, through an exit door, out into sunlight.

A bell clanged from the Disneyland Railroad station—a train was preparing to depart. Stukey quickened his pace and climbed aboard.

"Next stop, Main Street, U.S.A.," the conductor boomed.

That's where Stukey got off, and exited the theme park.

As his motel shuttle bus pulled away, Stukey watched six police cars, lights flashing, race up to Disneyland's entrance.

Stukey burst into his motel room and switched on the TV set. CNN was breaking news about a Stukey sighting in Anaheim, California.

"Even as his paintings are being exhibited at the Museum of Modern Art in New York City, Willard Stukey is reported by eyewitnesses to be stalking Donald Duck in Disneyland," blared the TV.

"Jig's up," muttered Stukey. "Time to bail."

The artist stuffed his fedora beneath the bed mattress and quickly packed a bag. Then he visited the motel office.

"Checking out," he said to the clerk.

"So?" This was a scrawny, goateed twenty-two-year-old named Rex Lappin. He barely looked up from a half-eaten salami and cream cheese sandwich. "You paid cash, bye."

Stukey didn't budge. "I need a ride," he said.

Rex Lappin rolled his eyes. "The shuttle leaves on the hour."

"Not to Disneyland," said Stukey.

"Then you're plum out of luck, 'cos that's. . ." Lappin looked up and came face to face with a Hechler & Koch MPSKA4 9mm machine pistol.

"I think you're the one out of plums," said Stukey. "Where's your car?"

"Jeez! You're that Stukey guy, aren't you?"

Stukey smiled. "Yup. Now, shut up, stand up, and lead me to your car."

Lappin tossed the remainder of his sandwich aside. "You want my keys?"

"No, I want you to show me your car," said Stukey. "And remember, I've killed about fifty people so far. Makes no difference if I add you to the list."

"Okay, okay. Take it easy, man."

"I could use some money, too. How much cash you got in there?" Stukey waved his weapon at the cash register.

"Aw, shit, man. They'll think *I* took it."

"I'll pay you back," said Stukey.

"How in hell you gonna pay me back?"

"First off," Stukey re-pointed his gun at Lappin. "I'll give you the gift of life."

"What the hell's that mean?"

"It means I won't shoot you dead," said Stukey. "Second, I'll draw something for you."

"What?"

"Don't *what* me. It'll be worth a fortune one day. Now open that cash register."

Lappin hit a key. The register opened. He lifted a wad of twenties.

"Under the drawer," said Stukey.

Lappin lifted the drawer to expose a smattering of fifty and one hundred dollar bills.

"That's much better." Stukey stuffed the bills into his pants pocket. "Let's go."

Stukey followed Lappin to a bright red, bottom-of-the-line Cherokee. Lappin unlocked the vehicle and held out his keys. "She's all I got in the world, man. Take care of her. I doubt I'm even insured for this kind of thing."

"Get in," said Stukey.

"What?"

"You're driving."

"Shit," said Lappin, "you're not taking me hostage, are you?"

"Nope. I just need someone to drive."

"Drive where?"

"I haven't decided yet," said Stukey.

"But you're not gonna kill me, right?"

"Not unless you don't get in the car."

Lappin jumped in. Stukey climbed in beside him.

"You know," Lappin started the engine, "I want to be a writer. Mind if I interview you?"

"Interview me?"

"Yeah. I'll ask you some questions, you answer them. This could be my lucky break."

"Are you nuts or something?" said Stukey. "Who do you write for?"

"Right now, I'm just freelance. I've had a couple pieces published in an Anaheim weekly. But this . . . man, I could sell this to *anyone*, get my career launched. What do you say?"

Stukey reflected on this. "Yeah, why not. You can interview me."

"Cool! Which way, man?"

"How far is Mexico from here?" asked Stukey.

"A couple hours."

"What's the border like?"

"Going in's easy," said Lappin. "It's coming back that's a bitch."

Stukey shook his head. "Nah, I hated Spanish in grade

school. Head north."

"You got it, man."

Lappin steered his Cherokee into traffic, then onto the Santa Ana Freeway.

Stukey switched the radio on and scanned. Every station was reporting that the Mickey Murder Manhunt had focused on Orange County.

Lappin slapped the steering wheel and hooted.

"What are you yelping about?" demanded Stukey.

"Everyone in the whole country is looking for you, and here you are, man—sitting right next to me! *I'm* the fucking story!"

"*I'm* the fucking story," said Stukey. "You're just a side dish of puke. Now, you gonna start this interview, or what?"

"I really should tape it," said Lappin.

"Why?"

"Everyone'll think I made it up."

"Do you have a tape machine with you?"

"I could stop and buy one."

"Too much trouble," said Stukey. "I'd have to go in with you, make sure you don't escape and call the cops."

"And lose this scoop? Give me a fucking break, man!"

"No, no, no. We're not stopping nowhere. If you want to ask questions, start asking. I'll write you a note that says it really happened."

"Would you?"

"Yeah. I'll combine it with that drawing I said I'd do, in payment for this ride."

"Okay, here goes: Did you really kill all those people."

"Yup, I did."

"Why?"

"It was the only way I could make the world aware of my art."

"Um, you don't mind me playing devil's advocate for a minute, do you?" Lappin glanced down at Stukey's gun.

"Ask anything you want." Stukey grinned. "If I don't like the question, I'll just shoot you."

"You're kidding, right?"

Stukey shrugged. "Take your chances."

"Okay, next question. And just give me a hint if you don't like where I'm taking this, huh? Is your art really worth all those lives?"

"Good question," said Stukey.

"So you've thought about it?"

"Of course. You think I'd go out and shoot a bunch of people without thinking about why?"

Lappin glanced sideways. "I come into this without any preconceived thoughts, man. I'm just asking." He paused. "So, how is it your art is worth all the suffering you've caused people?"

"Do you have any idea how many people were alive when van Gogh painted?" said Stukey. "Millions. But how many of them do we remember? Not many. Only a handful. You know why? Because only art prevails, that's why. It's the only thing mankind leaves behind that means anything. If fifty people got gunned down in the late 1800s, would we even care today? We wouldn't even *know*, let alone care. But if van Gogh had not been discovered... *that* would be a disaster."

"Are you comparing yourself to van Gogh?"

"My art speaks for itself," huffed Stukey. "Comparisons are irrelevant. Van Gogh died believing he failed everybody, including himself." Stukey shook his head. "Such a goddamn shame. Makes me wanna cry."

"But is that any reason to kill people?" posed Lappin.

"I had to," snapped Stukey. "No one was paying any attention. My act of violence made them sit up, take notice. Sometimes desperate measures are necessary."

"Killing people?"

"You have a hang-up about that?"

"Like, me and society in general, man."

Stukey looked straight ahead, annoyed by this simpleton. Maybe he *should* just blow him away. "People die," Stukey fumed, "but art lasts forever. Look around you." Stukey gestured 180 degrees with his machine pistol. "Everyone you see will be dead in a hundred years. Everyone. And most of humanity is scum anyway. We're in a state of decay from our first breath, feasted upon my microbes. We hurt each other. We kill each other. This car will be scrap metal in a tenth of that time. The stores you see, they'll all get replaced by even uglier architecture. Architecture gets worse all the time. And nothing stays the same. Except art. Art that great artists leave behind. The purity of it."

Stukey closed his eyes and prayed aloud. "Catherine of Bologna, none so pure as you." He opened his eyes. "The picture I'm gonna draw for you will be around for your great-grandchildren to look at—or sell for a college education. Art is the currency of the super-rich. You get it now?"

"Uh, yeah, man." Lappin scratched his bearded chin. "Sort of."

"Good. Now let's take a break from this interview stuff and listen to what they're saying on the radio. My life sorta depends on it."

29

Jeff Dalkin was eating pasta in Harry Cipriani, at the base of the Sherry-Netherland Hotel on Fifth Avenue, when his cell phone whistled. "Yeah–what?"

It was R. James Cloverland, calling to say that Willard Stukey had been spotted at Disneyland in California.

"You see," said Cloverland, "you went to all this trouble to hold an exhibition and it didn't matter. He's still stalking Donald Duck."

"Maybe he hasn't heard?"

"You kidding?" exclaimed Cloverland. "There are only two stories today: Stukey's exhibition and a Stukey sighting."

"Okay, maybe it's not really him in Disneyland?"

"Who else–male, caucasian, mid-30s–who else would be looking for Donald Duck in Disneyland without a kid?"

"A hoaxster, a copy-catter?"

"You're grasping at straws," said Cloverland.

"If I am, I learned it at the Bureau–butt-bashing bargsters, blow me."

"If you didn't have Tourette's I'd hang up."

"If I didn't have Tourette's," said Dalkin, "I'd have your job and I'd be hanging up on you. Lo mein."

30

"POLICE ARE SEARCHING the Anaheim motel room where Willard Stukey has been hiding for the last several days," announced a radio newsreader.

"Shit, that was quick!" said Stukey, completing a sketch of Rex Lappin at the wheel.

"Police believe Stukey may have kidnapped a motel employee named Rex Lappin. . . ."

"Is that you?" said Stukey.

"Yeah, man! I'm on the radio!"

". . . and that Stukey is using Lappin's red Cherokee to escape from the area. . ."

"They got that right," said Stukey.

". . . California license plate number. . . ."

"Aw, shit," Stukey protested. "Why did they have to go and do that?"

"What now?" said Lappin.

"Pull over," said Stukey.

"Over where? We're on a freeway, man!"

"I don't care. Pull onto the shoulder."

"Why?"

"You're getting out."

"You're gonna leave me on the freeway?"

"It's that or kill you." Stukey shrugged. "Take your pick."

"I'll bail," said Lappin. "What about that drawing you were going to do for me? Proof that we met?"

"You heard the friggin' radio. You don't need proof anymore. Now pull over!"

Lappin steered his Cherokee onto the shoulder and slowed to a halt.

"See ya–bye." Stukey pointed his gun.

Lappin jerked the door handle and climbed out.

"Hold on." Stukey tore a page from his sketchbook, crumpled it into a ball and tossed it out the door after Lappin. "A deal's a deal." Then he shifted into the driver's seat, thrust the gear into drive and screeched off.

31

ON SUNDAY, THE *New York Times* published a review of the Willard Stukey Exhibition at MoMA. By-lined Randall Twining III, the review was spread over two pages.

"I went to Willard Stukey's exhibition hoping to God his work would be mediocre," wrote Twining, "and that it would not merit a review—good or bad—in this newspaper. Unfortunately—and I say this because the artist has admitted on national television to murdering over fifty people—Stukey's canvases are not mediocre, but marvelous. I am not over-stating the matter when I say that Willard Stukey may well be the Vincent van Gogh of his generation. He is, without doubt, an artistic genius, the likes of which this world produces about once a century."

The review continued on in this rapturous way.

Michael Eisner flung the arts section across his Pierre Hotel suite. "How can they laud that murderer?" Disney's chairman stormed. "He's terrorizing my theme parks! Attendance is down fifty percent!"

Jeff Dalkin sat stiffly in a desk chair. "It's everything we could have hoped for," he said softly. "Stukey's conditions are met. He no longer has a reason to kill Donald Duck."

"Donald Duck *cannot* be killed!" Eisner raged. "And if what you say is true, why the hell was this maniac in my park yesterday, looking for Donald Duck, goddammit?! And now the FBI has lost him again."

"As of this morning," Dalkin spoke calmly, *"both* conditions are met. Garbanza beans. Stukey got what he wanted. Way beyond his expectations, I'd guess. The motel guy he kidnapped said Stukey wasn't interested in fleeing to Mexico. Splooging spics. That can only mean he plans to stick around and give himself up. The game is over. Actually, lo mein."

"This isn't a game," snapped Eisner.

"To Stukey it is. He just won. The *New York Times*–barfing bargsters–has acclaimed him a great artist. That's all he ever wanted. Actually, Floto, lo mein."

"Would you shut the hell up?"

32

Monday at nine p.m., Larry King faced two guests on CNN's *Larry King Live*: Nathaniel Sugarman and Randall Twining III.

"Could it be," Larry King posed, "that this admitted murderer, Willard Stukey, is truly the van Gogh of our time?"

The curator of MoMA nodded enthusiastically. "Irrefutably so. Perhaps better."

"Better? But he's a cold-blooded killer," said King.

"The downside of creative genius," Sugarman responded. "Remember, van Gogh sliced off part of his ear and spent time in an insane asylum."

"But the suffering Stukey has caused." King shook his head.

"Should we condemn fabulous works of art because the artist possesses a psychopathic mind?" said Sugarman.

"So what do you propose we do with him when and if he's caught?" posed King. "This one's for you, Randall. Should Stukey get the electric chair?"

"It would be a crime to prevent an artist of this calibre

from producing new works of art," replied Twining. "If van Gogh had murdered someone at age nineteen and then been executed as a result, consider the cultural void that would now exist."

Willard Stukey watched this exchange in disbelief inside a Santa Fe, New Mexico, hotel room. After ditching Rex Lappin on the freeway, Stukey had abandoned the Cherokee and taxied to LA's Greyhound bus station. The light and space of the desert–to which he had been so attracted a few days earlier aboard Amtrak–had whistled his name.

Stukey scribbled Larry King's 800 call-in number on a motel notepad and left his room in search of a public telephone.

"Willard, you're live," said Larry King. "Willard? Are you there?"

"I'm here."

"What's your question?" asked King.

"I don't have a question. I just want to tell those two jackasses to quit mocking me."

"Mocking you?"

"All this van Gogh crap," Stukey drawled. "You think I'm an idiot?"

"What do you mean, Willard?" King wiped his spectacles.

"Ain't it obvious, Larry? It's all a ruse–to get me to turn myself in. It's only making me madder'n a hornet's nest on fire."

"Wait a minute, you. . .?"

"No, you wait a minute, Larry. I don't take kindly to

being made fun of. I think I'll just add those two smug bastards to my hit list."

"You're threatening to kill Nathaniel Sugarman and Randall Twining on my broadcast?" King contorted his face in astonishment for dramatic effect.

"The art world would be better off without 'em," said Stukey.

"But they *love* your work, Willard! They think you are a creative genius!"

"You see, this is just what I'm talking about, Larry. I think I'll add you to my list. too."

"You're threatening to kill *me*?"

"Damn right I am."

"But . . . but. . . ."

"Don't but me," said Stukey. "You and those clowns sitting next to you can suck my paintbrush. And that goes for Mr. Floto, too."

"Where are you calling from, Willard?" asked Larry King.

"You really want to know?"

"Yes."

"I'm inside your studio," growled Stukey.

Even under a coat of pancake, Larry King's face whitened; his two guests shifted with discomfort.

"Just kidding, Larry," said Stukey. "But you never know. See ya–bye."

"Did you hear that?" hollered Michael Eisner. "That idiot doesn't believe they think he's a great artist. Goddammit, Dalkin—you overdid it!"

Dalkin shrugged. "Bargs."

"What now?" demanded Eisner.

"Let me call my guy at the Bureau—bonehead baloney-beating butt-wipes. Maybe he's heard something." Dalkin picked up a cordless phone and touch-keyed R. James Cloverland's home number. "Jim? Are you watching Larry King?"

"Watching isn't believing," said Cloverland.

"Did they trace him?"

"Nope. Only that producer Scrupula's line has a trace on it."

"So he could be anywhere?"

"Anywhere within forty-eight hours' ground travel of LA," said Cloverland.

"You've got to be kidding?"

"Me? You're the joker in this thing. A MoMA exhibition, a *New York Times* review. And this lunatic says he's adding the museum curator, the review writer *and* Larry King to his list. Way to go, buddy!"

Dalkin disconnected, re-focusing his attention on *Larry King Live*.

"How much do you think Stukey's paintings are worth, Nathaniel?" asked Larry.

"It's difficult to estimate a price," said MoMA's curator.

"Take a guess," Larry prodded. "Ball park."

"Minimum, half-a-million dollars," said Sugarman.

"For your twenty-painting collection?"

"No," said Sugarman, "half-a-million *each*."

Dalkin pressed redial on the phone.

R. James Cloverland answered.

"Jim? By my calculations, you still have ninety-eight

paintings in your. . ."

"Don't get any new ideas," Cloverland cut him off. "If Stukey wants his paintings, he's going to have to come get them in person."

"I was just thinking that maybe you and me should open an art gallery and . . ." Dalkin looked up to see Michael Eisner glaring at him. "Just kidding. Lo mein." He disconnected the phone and re-focused on the TV set.

"How did this exhibition come about?" asked Larry King.

"A represenative of Michael Eisner came to see me. . ." said Sugarman.

"Oh my God!" howled Eisner.

"Shit, oh, shit," said Dalkin. "Shit, shit, shit. Lo mein."

". . . of course," continued Sugarman, "MoMA had no intention of giving into the demands of a murderer, even at the request of the Walt Disney Company. But this . . . detective, I think that's what he is, a private detective named Jeff Dalkin. . ."

"He looks just like Bruce Willis," Randall Twining interjected. "He came to see me, too."

Eisner switched the power off by remote and turned on Dalkin. "You're fired!" he shouted. "Get out!"

"Bargs." Dalkin smirked, shrugged and split. He walked to Soup Burg, corner of Madison and Seventy-third Street, for a Smother Burger and a Coke.

Dalkin was contemplating dessert, maybe lemon meringue pie, when his cell phone whistled. "Shit, this is how it started," he muttered, flipping open his StarTac, expecting Michael Eisner's voice. "Yeah–what? Blow me."

It wasn't Eisner. It was a former CIA spymaster who doled out rich clients with wacky assignments to former colleagues from the intelligence community.

Was Dalkin available for a job?

Yeah, Dalkin was.

Could Dalkin do lunch in DC tomorrow?

Yeah, Dalkin could.

33

HARVEY KIMBACH WAS waiting in a booth in Martin's Tavern, corner of N Street and Wisconsin Avenue in the heart of Georgetown. Kimbach was tall and lean, a thick mane of gray hair. He waved.

Jeff Dalkin strode over. "Hey, Harve."

The presumed appearance of Bruce Willis caused furtive glances, whispering and finger-pointing among patrons inside the popular eatery, duly noted with unease by the former spymaster.

"How do you live like this?" Kimbach asked.

Dalkin smirked like Bruce Willis.

"It would drive me crazy." Kimbach opened the menu. "I recommend crab cakes."

"Crab cakes," said Dalkin. "Floto, lo mein."

"I heard your name on CNN last night," said Kimbach.

Dalkin put his hand over his eyes.

"That's what gave me the idea to phone you." Kimbach paused to sip his vodka martini. "I've had a number of calls from a multi-millionaire with a personal problem. The guys

I usually give stuff to are occupied this week. It's yours if you want it."

"Go on."

"The client is an Indian from India, resident here in the United States. In Pennsylvania. He is related to the Wali of Swat. . . ."

"The what?"

"The Wali of Swat. Provincial Indian royalty. His name is Mark Alouwahlia. Made his money in electronics. About a hundred million."

"Wali of Swat," said Dalkin. "What's his problem?"

"No, he's a cousin to the Wali of Swat. Mark was divorced from his American wife three years ago. They had two children, a boy and girl, ages six and three. The court awarded joint custody. About four months ago his ex-wife disappeared with the kids. They haven't been seen since. He wants someone to find them. And he's offering a million dollar reward."

Dalkin arched his eyebrows. "Wali of Swat, Wali of Swat."

"No, his cousin."

"I know I know I know I know." Dalkin stamped his right foot four times, then palmed his knee to hold his leg in place. "Tourette's."

"Ah, yes," said Kimbach.

"A million bucks?"

Kimbach nodded. "That's what he says."

"Why don't you do it yourself? Crab cakes, Floto, lo mein, Wali of Swat."

"I prefer to hand out assignments like this one. And take a commission. If you want the assignment, my cut is ten percent."

"Is this Wali of Swat cousin willing to cough up some up-front dough?"

"You'll have to ask him. If you're interested, I'll set up a meeting—just you and him—in Philadelphia."

"Why the hell not? Bargs."

"He's anxious to get started," said Kimbach. "I'll find a phone and call him now." The former spymaster lifted his butt.

"Here." Dalkin dug into his pocket. "Use my cell phone."

Kimbach accepted the StarTac, looked at it. "How do these things work?"

Dalkin helped Kimbach connect to Mark Alouwahlia. The two men chatted. Kimbach cupped the phone. "You want to go up today for a late afternoon meeting?"

34

D ALKIN BOARDED A Metroliner at Union Station and Amtrakked north. Halfway to Philly, his cell phone whistled.

"Yeah–what?" Dalkin answered.

"This is Willard Stukey." said a voice.

"Funny, Cloverland. What do you want?"

"I'm Willard Stukey, successful artist. I heard your name on *Larry King* last night. I got your number from information in New York."

Dalkin recognized the voice now. "Jesus Christ, it *is* you. What the hell do you want? Crab cakes, lo mein, Wali of Swat."

"Huh?"

"You heard me, you crazy mutherfucker. Are you calling to put *me* on your hit list? Floto, bargs, lo mein."

"What?"

"I got you into MoMA, I got you the review you wanted in the *Times*–and I don't care if you think it's a joke–those intellectual nitwits really love your paintings."

"Really?"

"Yeah, really. And what do I get? A big kick in the ass.

So you want to add my name to your hit list? Go right ahead, you murdering jerk. Try to take me on!"

"Uh, no, that's not what I want," said Stukey.

"No? Then what?"

"I want you to be my agent."

"Say what?"

"If what they're saying on TV is true, my paintings are worth a lot of money, guy. I can't represent myself. Aside from being wanted for murder, it's not the right thing for an artist to do. I need an agent. And since you were so good n'all getting my paintings recognized, it might as well be you."

"Are you nuts? Wait a minute—you *are* nuts. In any case, the FBI—fornicating fart-licking flat-foots—took all your paintings away."

"Damn." Stukey paused. "So I'll paint more."

"Are you serious?"

"Damn serious."

"So you're not going to kill anybody else?"

"No need."

"What about threatening to shoot that fancy-pants Sugarman, and Randall Twining, and Larry King from CNN—turds and maggots?"

"That was poetry," said Stukey.

"So you're a poet *and* an artist?"

"Painting and poetry are bedmates," said Stukey. "So, you interested or what?"

"I'll think about it," said Dalkin. "Where can I reach you?"

"I'll call you, guy. See ya—bye."

"Hello? Hello?" Dalkin flipped his phone shut, and reclined his seat to reflect on this strange new development.

35

THE THING THAT surprised Jeff Dalkin most about Mark Alouwahlia was his grotesque ugliness. He was a hulk of a man, with hunched shoulders and an Indian-ness contrasted by a buttoned-down Brooks Brothers costume. His eyes bulged, his beard was spotty, his cheeks pock-marked, and everything was clustered around an acquiline nose. It was as if God had made this guy spectacularly hideous—with an odor of stale, three-day old garlic—as a warning for others to move on or beware.

Alouwahlia's unsightliness was surpassed only by his arrogance—conveyed first with body language, then by the condescending manner he used on the pretty cocktail lounge waitress inside the Four Seasons Hotel in the City of Brotherly Love. Alouwahlia actually snapped his fingers to hasten her attention, then quickly took control, ordering a beer for Dalkin and a kir royale for himself.

"Harve Kimbach told me you're looking for your ex-wife," Dalkin opened.

"Not my ex-wife, the bitch," Alouwahlia bristled. "My

children. The bitch can go to hell. I want my children back. She abducted them. A crime. She has broken the law, yes. She violated the court. She will go to prison for kidnapping my children." He paused. "She's a nymphomaniac," he added.

Dalkin nodded. There was nothing worse than acrimonious divorces. Except mass killers. How did Dalkin ever get into this business? Already, he did not like this Indian. Even if he was cousin of the Wali of Swat, whatever *that* was.

"You must find my children and return them to me," said Alouwahlia. "For this I am offering a very large reward." The Indian popped a slim briefcase and drew out a manila file folder. "I have names, social security numbers, passport numbers, addresses of relatives. . . ."

"That's good," Dalkin cut in. "And I'm going need this file *if* I decide to take this assignment."

"I am offering one million dollars," said Alouwahlia, eyes bugging, as if Dalkin should get down on his knees and lick the Indian's hand-sewn J. P. Tod mocassins for giving him this opportunity.

"Yeah, I heard," said Dalkin. "Problem is, I never work on spec. Sleuthing takes time and expenses. I'm not saying I don't like success fees, it's just that I'm going to need something at the front end to get cranked up. Call it a draw from the success fee."

"How much draw?"

"Twenty grand."

Alouwahlia laughed sourly.

Dalkin discerned this to be a negotiating tactic. "Non negotiable," he added, staring the Indian down.

"And for this you guarantee return of my children?"

"Nope. There are no guarantees in this business. Ever. Trust me." Dalkin winked. "I'll find 'em. But that's *all* I can do. To get them returned you'll need a lawyer to jump a few legal hurdles."

"But this bitch has broken the law," Alouwahlia wailed. "They should arrest her."

"If your ex-wife has done this right," said Dalkin, "she's no longer in the United States. She'll probably be in an English-speaking country like Canada or Australia or New Zealand."

"How do you know this?" Alouwahlia arched his bushy eyebrows as if maybe Dalkin and his ex-wife were in cahoots.

"You're not the first spouse to lose his kids like this. There's a rhythm to how it works. I know how to break the code and find your children. The rest is up to your lawyer."

A waitress delivered libations.

Alouwahlia picked up his glass and sipped. "Hey!" he beckoned the waitress back. "It's too sweet. Take it away and get me another."

Alouwahlia wanted to be an American, but he knew that when people looked at him, they saw an Indian dressed in Brookies togs. The French had an expression for it, something about not being comfortable inside your own skin.

"You're from Bombay, aren't you?" said Dalkin.

"Bangalore," replied Alouwahlia. "I'm an American citizen," he added. "You look familiar. Have we met before?"

"I doubt it." Dalkin pulled a pen from his inside coat

pocket. "Think about what I said. I don't have a business card. I'll write my number . . ."

"Will you find my children?" Alouwahlia blurted with imploring eyes. There was some humanity in there, somewhere.

"I can find anyone, anywhere," Dalkin winked. "Lo mein."

Alouwahlia dipped into the gusseted pocket of his briefcase and plucked a checkbook. "Twenty thousand dollars?" he said.

Dalkin nodded. "Yep."

Alouwahlia scribbled. "An advance on my reward. But since you will only find, not return, my children, my reward must be half. Five hundred thousand dollars."

Dalkin shook his head. "The deal is one million dollars—blow me—for finding your children. That's why I trained up here. If that's not the deal, do it yourself."

Alouwahlia folded his arms and glared at Dalkin.

A waitress tippy-toed over with a fresh kir royale.

Alouwahlia sipped, grunted his approval. "You find my children," Alouwahlia pronounced. "When you do, my full reward will be paid."

36

D‌ALKIN'S CELLULAR BATTERY was almost dead, so he opted for a public phone inside Philadelphia's Thirtieth Street Station and touch-keyed a number.

"He's just leaving," said a secretary.

"Catch him," said Dalkin.

A minute passed.

"Cloverland," said R. James Cloverland, assistant director of the FBI.

"Jim, it's me. Dalkin. Free for dinner?"

Sushi-Ko, Washington's oldest sushi bar, was bustling at 7:30 p.m. Heads turned when Dalkin swaggered in. First a hush, followed by the inevitable whispering.

"Yeah, he's in town shooting a movie called *Lo Mein*," said one knowledgable diner.

R. James Cloverland arrived a few minutes later and sat opposite Dalkin. "So, what's so damn important?" He probed Dalkin's eyes. "Does Eisner have another big idea? That sonofabitch called my director today."

"It's got nothing to do with me. Ei . . . oh, shit. . . Ei. . . fuck . . . Ei-yi-yi-yi!" Dalkin sang like a Mexican mariachi on a sweltering night in downtown Tijuana.

Cloverland covered his eyes.

Dalkin took a deep breath. "My boss—nazi schwinehund, blow a fart—fired me."

"Why?" Cloverland was genuinely surprised.

Dalkin shrugged. "Things aren't going his way. Lo mein, crab cakes, Wali of Swat."

"What?"

Dalkin steadied himself, both hands on the table. "It's the Tourette's. I need a drink."

"Eisner didn't know you have Tourette's?"

"No, no, no. He knew. Knows. Bargs. Floto. Lo mein."

"Okay, calm down." Cloverland signaled for a waitress. "Can we order some drinks? I'd like a Japanese beer. My friend will have . . ." Cloverland pointed his thumb across the table.

"Lo mein," said Dalkin.

"This Japanese restaurant," said the Japanese waitress. "No lo mein. We have suba noodle."

"I'll have hot sake," said Dalkin. "Real hot."

The waitress departed.

"I heard from Stukey," said Dalkin.

"*What?*" Cloverland was certain he had mis-heard.

"Stukey called me."

"*Willard* Stukey?"

Dalkin nodded. "Of course. What other Stukey?"

"He *called* you?" Cloverland was flabbergasted. "Why?" he finally gasped.

"He wants me to be his agent."

"His agent?"

"To represent his paintings."

"Is he nuts?" boomed Cloverland.

"Criminally insane is probably a better term."

"I must be missing something," said Cloverland. "How did—?"

"Those turd twins—Sugarman and Twining—talked about me on *Larry King*, and. . ."

"Ohhhh, okay." Cloverland whistled at the ceiling. "I get it now. So he phoned you?"

"Yep. A few hours ago." Dalkin held out his cell phone. "Calls to my listed landline are forwarded automatically."

"I don't suppose he gave you a number to reach him at?" asked Cloverland.

"Wishful thinking. Bargs. He said he's going to call again."

"But you're not working for Eisner anymore?"

Dalkin shrugged. "I told you, he fired me."

"I don't understand." Cloverland threw up his arms. "So?"

"It's simple," said Dalkin. "I have a legal right to Stukey's paintings now. You've got to hand them over."

"I can't believe this," said Cloverland, hunching forward. "Eisner fired you so you're taking *Stukey's* side?"

Dalkin winked. "I can make Stukey *think* that."

"I don't follow."

"Yeah, that's the Bureau—back-assed bug-eyed boogerheads—in you. If we do this right, I'll gain Stukey's confidence and get him to meet me. Unless you have a better plan for catching him?"

Cloverland looked away.

"What did your director tell Ei . . . goddammit! . . . Ei . . . shit! Ei-yi-yi-yi!" Dalkin sang like a Mexican mariachi on mescaline.

"Our director said we're doing everything we could," said Cloverland.

"Which translates to jerking off," Dalkin retorted. "Looks like I'm your only hope."

"Why don't you take this back to Eisner? He can afford to pay you better."

"No, no, no. I'm not going back to that, that, that . . . oh, man, where's Tourette's when you need it? Nazi schwinehund! Plus there's something I need from you in exchange."

"Uh-oh." Cloverland closed his eyes.

"It's no big deal. I've been hired by a guy whose ex-wife split with the kids—curry-quaffing cunt-head. I just want you to run it through the system, see what turns up. Bargs, Floto, lo mein."

Cloverland nodded. "I can do that. You've got a name?"

"Yep. And birthdates and social security numbers. Here." Dalkin produced an index card with vital statistics for two parents, two children. From Alouwahlia's file.

Cloverland tucked the card into his shirt pocket. "What's the next step?"

"Stukey's supposed to phone me back. I'll tell him I thought about it and, sure, I want to be his agent. I already told him to forget about all the paintings in his studio. He says he's going to paint more pictures. That means a transfer, from him to me, has to take place. So I'll try to wangle a meeting with him."

The waitress arrived with beer and hot sake. "I take order now?"

"Tuna roll," said Cloverland.

"Tekka maki," noted the waitress.

"Tekka maki, tekka maki," said Dalkin.

"Two tekka maki." said the waitress, turning.

"No," said Dalkin. "Tekka maki, crab cakes, lo mein."

The waitress turned around. "No lo mein, no crab cake. Two tekka maki, okay?"

"No," said Dalkin. "Oh, shit, forget it."

She did.

Dalkin looked at Cloverland. "What the hell's tekka maki?"

"Raw tuna, rolled with rice in seaweed."

"Tekka maki, tekka maki, crab cakes, lo mein, Floto, Wali of Swat–goddammit!" Trembling, Dalkin poured himself a small cup of sake and sipped. Somehow, a drink always helped.

Cloverland eyed Dalkin cautiously. "So what's next?"

"I'll catch the last shuttle home to New York–niggers and kikes. I'll recharge my cell phone battery, stay by the phone, wait for Stukey's call. Meantime, you call me when you've got info on my missing children case."

37

WILLARD STUKEY SAT in the desert north of Santa Fe, New Mexico, furiously painting foothills and mountains, sky and desert. Painting like he'd never painted before: thick, swirling brushstrokes from a palette far bolder than usual. It was as if both he and nature, during their first open air experience together, had been sprinkled with magic dust that intensified space and light, turning it electric, magnetic, concentric. . . .

Stukey created a unique interpretation of the cosmos, and how it related to this patch of desert, mountains, and sunlight at the center of the universe. He painted like a man possessed—possessed by hue, saturation, and tone; an artist completely absorbed by the elements. And, after fourteen hours—from sunrise to sunset—his soul soared. Exhiliration. Stukey could see immediately that his exhibition of abstract expressionist works at MoMA was nothing compared to this new batch of painted canvases.

Later, back at his motel, Stukey pulsated with excitement. He had to tell someone. His would-be agent, perhaps.

Jeff Dalkin was into the first few minutes of CNN's ten o'clock news—about Willard Stukey, what else?—when his phone rang.

"Yeah—what?" Dalkin answered.

"It's me, Willard Stukey." The artist's voice bubbled with enthusiasm.

"How are you?"

"I've had a good day, real good," said Stukey. "The desert . . ." he could not help himself. "It's so . . . so . . . *vibrant*. I'm painting again. So, have you decided?"

"Here's my problem, Willard." Dalkin did not wish to appear too anxious. "In some quarters, this might be construed as aiding and abetting."

"No," said Stukey. "You have to separate me from my art. *I* killed Mickey Mouse and others. I don't deny it. But my *art* is pure—guilty of nothing. I strive for purity. For honesty. There is nothing so pure, or as honest, as my painting."

"Okay, okay," said Dalkin. "I'm in."

"Really? Outstanding! I'll get back to you. See ya—bye."

Dalkin touch-keyed R. James Cloverland's home number. "Stukey called again," Dalkin blurted. "He's painting the desert."

"Which one?" Cloverland was excited.

"He didn't say. Does this jibe with anything you're hearing?"

"We're not hearing anything," said Cloverland. "A new thought occured to Cloverland. "Do you have Caller ID?"

"Nope."

"Damn! We need to send someone up there and put a

tracer on your phone."

"Before you do," said Dalkin, "make sure you got what I need on those missing children."

38

Dalkin sat watching two agents from the FBI's technical support staff toy with his telephone. "What if I get the call on my cell phone?" he asked.

"You mean on call-forward?" said a technician. "Same difference."

The phone rang.

"It's coming from headquarters." A technician scratched his head.

Dalkin picked up. "Yeah—what?"

"Okay," said Cloverland. "I got some information on that case you're working."

Dalkin glimpsed a technician listening in on earphones. "Hey, you going to listen to every fucking call I get?"

The technician shrugged. "How do we know it's him unless we're listening?"

"You think he's in your headquarters?" Dalkin asked sarcastically. "Never mind, he *could* be there and you bozos *still* wouldn't catch him."

"I heard that," said Cloverland.

"I'll shuttle down for a face-to-face," said Dalkin. "Lo mein."

39

"Here's what we know." Cloverland looked over his desk at Dalkin. "Your client, Mark Alouwahlia, filed a criminal complaint against his ex-wife for the abduction of their two children. There's a warrant out for her arrest. The Bureau is in on this because she's suspected of crossing state lines. Between you and me, the Bureau isn't actively looking for her."

"Status quo, eh?" said Dalkin.

"No." Cloverland didn't smile. "We don't have a lot of sympathy for this kind of thing." He pushed a glossy eight-by-twelve color photograph across the desk.

"Who . . . ?" Dalkin didn't recognize the swollen, discolored face.

"The former Mrs. Alouwahlia," said Cloverland.

"Shit!"

"We see a lot of cases like this," said Cloverland. "And when we do, we tend toward turning a blind eye. The missus and her kids are better off without this creep."

"Do you have *any* idea where they are?"

Cloverland shrugged. "You really want to return them to this guy?"

"We're talking a million bucks—blow me. All I'm supposed to do is find them. I'm guessing they're in another country, where he faces a whole new set of hurdles."

Cloverland nodded. "You're probably right. That's another reason we don't spend a lot of man hours on this kind of stuff. There is one lead I can give you."

Dalkin edged in on Cloverland's desk.

"We know of a woman who runs an underground railroad for abused wives," continued Cloverland. "She tells them how to get new ID, transfer money, and set up a new home overseas."

"You think that's who Alouwahlia's ex-wife used?"

"They all do."

"How do they hear about her?"

"Shelters." Cloverland yawned. "There's a grapevine for this kind of thing."

"So why don't you bug her phones and catch these child abductors before they split?"

"You kidding? We privately *applaud* what she does. Charleston, South Carolina. That's where she lives." Cloverland pushed a piece of note-paper across his desk. "Her name, address, phone number."

A phone clanged. Cloverland picked up, listened, put it down, got up. "Disney's making an announcement of some kind." He walked around his desk and switched the TV on.

"A spokesman for Disney chairman Michael Eisner," said a CNN reporter standing outside Disney Studios in Burbank, California, "has just announced that the Walt Disney Company is doubling their reward for information leading to the arrest and conviction of Willard Stukey. The reward now stands at two million dollars."

Cloverland whistled.

Dalkin absorbed this. "Hey, that's me," he said.

"Where?" Cloverland peered into the television set.

"No, *I'm* the one with the information that's going to catch Stukey. *I* should get the two million dollar–blow me–reward."

Cloverland shrugged. "That's between you and Eisner."

"Not only," said Dalkin. "I'm going to need you to corroborate this."

"What say we catch Stukey first," said Cloverland, "then worry about who did what."

"Shh!" Dalkin pointed to the TV set.

"This reward," added the CNN correspondent, "does not apply to employees of the Walt Disney Company, nor their relatives, nor former employees."

"That nazi schwinehund!" hollered Dalkin. "Floto, bargs, crab cakes, tekka maki, Wali of Swat, lo mein!"

"Poetic," Cloverland commented.

"You think it's poetic that Ei-yi-yi-yi. . . !" Dalkin sang like a Mexican mariachi passing a kidney stone, ". . . that he's cutting me out?"

"No," Cloverland deadpanned. "Your reaction to it."

"Fuck you, you asshole," Dalkin fumed.

"What'd you say?" Cloverland stiffened.

"Tourette's!"

"I don't think that was Tourette's." Cloverland narrowed his eyes.

Dalkin's cell phone whistled.

"You think it's him?" Cloverland's brows arched.

"We'll know in a second." Dalkin flipped his phone open. "Yeah–what?"

"It's me. Willard Stukey."

"Hey, Willard." Dalkin made eye contact with Cloverland, trying to sound low-key. "What's up?"

Cloverland scribbled a note and held it up: KEEP HIM TALKING!

Dalkin covered the mouthpiece. "Duh."

"It's just so incredible," Stukey said.

"What is—that reward offered by Ei . . . Ei . . . Ei-yi-yi-yi! Godammit! Are you talking about the reward?"

"What reward?"

"Disney—donkey dicks—they're offering a two million-dollar—blow me—reward for your capture."

"So what?" Stukey chuckled. "That's about what four of my paintings are worth. You're better off as my agent."

"Damn right. That goddam sonofabitch has made me ineligible for the reward. That's another reason you've got yourself an agent, Willard." Dalkin found the passion needed to seal this sucker. "We really should meet and plan a marketing strategy."

"I'm not ready to meet yet," said Stukey.

"That's cool. Take your time, Willard. We can start by strategizing over the phone. When do I get to see your new work?"

"It's drying now. I use a real lot of paint. Takes a week, at least, to dry. I'll send you a few pictures. That would be the way to start, I guess. I send you a few pictures, you deal them. What's your address?"

Dalkin recited his address in New York. "What are your paintings of?" Dalkin asked.

"Landscapes, guy. Desert and mountains. Expressionist and impressionist rolled into one. My own invention. It's awesome out here."

Dalkin was tempted to ask just *where* out there, but thought better of it. And, anyway, a better idea occured to him.

"See ya–bye," said Stukey abruptly.

"He's gone." Dalkin flipped his phone shut.

Cloverland shook his head anxiously. "It wasn't enough time." He paced, awaiting word. A phone on his desk rang. Cloverland jumped on it, listened, hung it up. "It's a five-zero-five area code," said Cloverland. "New Mexico. The whole state is five-o-five."

Dalkin smiled. "In ten days, we'll be able to pinpoint exactly where he is."

"How's that?" Cloverland stroked his moustache.

"He's going to send me a couple of paintings. Landscapes. Get it? We'll be able to pinpoint his location by studying what he painted."

"Uh-huh, got it." But Cloverland suddenly had *his* own idea; one he decidely did not share with Dalkin.

40

"MRS. DENGROVE?" Dalkin spoke into a public telephone. "My name is Jeff Squallace and my sister needs your help."

"Yes?" It was a sweet voice, like marmalade.

"She split up from her live-in boyfriend–they have a daughter–and this guy just refuses to let go. He's following her everywhere and she's afraid."

"Where did you get my name?" Lucy Dengrove asked sweetly.

"The FBI ... forni ..." Dalkin bit his lip in an effort to stave off a Tourettic impulse. "Fornicating fatheads from fartville!"

"Excuse me?"

"No, excuse me, ma'am–please don't hang up–I have Tourette's syndrome."

"What's that?"

"I curse uncontrollably. In my case, certain words set me off."

"Oh. You said you got my name from the FBI?" Lucy

Dengrove's curiosity was piqued.

"That's right. They actually like what do you. Actually, actually."

"Really?"

"Truly. My sister actually needs to leave New York. Lo mein. But she's afraid this nutcase is going to stalk her wherever she moves to. She needs the kind of help she can't actually get from lawyers and police. Tekka maki."

"What is your sister's name?"

"Olivia Squallace."

"Ask your sister to call me herself and . . ."

"Hold on, I have her right here." Relieved, Dalkin handed the phone to Olivia Squallace, a risk analyst at Control Risks International who moonlighted as a roll-playing private dick. Like Dalkin, Squallace was ex-Bureau and anti-bureaucrat.

"Hi," said Olivia Squallace. "Mrs. Dengrove?" Squallace's voice quivered. "My brother says you might be able to help me."

"I need to know more about you first, dear," said the marmalade voice.

"Of course."

Questioned by Lucy Dengrove, Olivia Squallace recited her address, phone number, social security number, birth-date, daughter's name, and ex-boyfriend's name.

"Have you filed a complaint with the police?" asked a satiated Dengrove.

"He told me he'd kill me if I did that," murmured Squallace. "And I believe him. He also says he's going to kidnap my daughter and take her to South America." Squallace began to sob.

"Do you work?" asked Dengrove.

"I need to quit my job and move," replied a tearful Squallace.

"Can you take a day off and come down to Charleston?" Dengrove spoke consolingly.

"I'll do anything." Squallace blew her nose into a handkerchief. "May I bring my brother?"

"No," said Dengrove. "I find it preferable to deal one-on-one, women-talk. The first phase of getting away from a situation like yours is total secrecy, especially with family. When would you like to visit?"

"As soon as possible," Squallace whimpered. "I'm desperate."

41

R. JAMES CLOVERLAND personally phoned the SAC, or Special Agent-in-Charge, of the FBI field office in Albuquerque, New Mexico.

"Art supply stores," said Cloverland. "This Willard Stukey is buying art supplies somewhere in New Mexico. Copy his stat sheet with photos of him for every art supply store in the state."

"Do you know how many artists we have in New Mexico?" asked the SAC.

"Not really."

"A lot. Artists come from all over the country and settle here. That translates to quite a few art supply shops."

"That's not my problem anymore," said Cloverland. "It's *yours*. And make sure everyone who receives a stat sheet hears about Disney's two million dollar reward."

42

W‍ITHIN FORTY-EIGHT HOURS, Olivia Squallace had been to Charleston, consulted with Lucy Dengrove, and returned to New York City. Dalkin was waiting for her at Soup Burg, corner of Madison and Seventy-third.

Squallace sauntered in and sat down. "Piece of cake." She opened a compact case to check herself out, then glanced around. "I deserve La Grenouille, not this raunchy dive."

"Good burgers," said Dalkin. "Since 1949. I recommend the Smother Burger."

A waiter stood by, pencil poised over his order pad.

"Just coffee," said Squallace.

"Lemme have a Smother Burger Deluxe," said Dalkin. "And a Coke."

"The woman you're looking for is in Australia." Squallace checked her polished nails.

"Dengrove told you that?"

"Of course not." Squallace looked up. "Not in those words, anyway. Australia is the country she favors for resettling runaway women. She says she's had great success in

Australia and that's where I should go."

"Where in Australia?"

Squallace smiled. "Got that, too." She paused. "Western Australia. Perth."

Dalkin was impressed. "You're good, Squallace. Lo mein."

"Good thing I really have a daughter," said Squallace. "She checked." Squallace consulted a pocket notebook. "There are others like you in Perth—those were her exact words. She's even organized a social group of women she's helped move to Perth so they can give each other moral support."

"Excellent, Squallace. She didn't happen to give you names, addresses?"

Squallace shook her head. "No. She gave me detailed instructions on how to set up a new identity for myself. You know, the old trick of getting a U.S. passport in a false name by stealing the identity of someone about your age who died as a child. From that, a new social security number, driver's license, library card, and so on. She said introductions to others in Perth come later, once I'm there."

"Did she say if she stays in touch with the women she helps?"

"She didn't actually say that. But she must if she introduces them to each other."

"Actually, actually," said Dalkin. "Lo mein. Tekka maki. Wali of Swat. How? By phone?"

A waiter plunked a Smother Burger Deluxe in front of the salivating Dalkin.

"Maybe by phone," said Squallace. "Probably by e-mail."

"Oh, that's good," Dalkin chomped. "Did you actually get her e-mail call-sign?"

"Of course." Squallace took another peek at her notebook. "She also recommends liquidating everything. Home, car, furniture, the works–even personal effects. 'It's just baggage,' she said. The point is to start a new life from scratch. She says I should take a trip to Europe, fly to Paris or Rome, then train to Zurich and open a numbered Swiss account."

"Any specific bank?" Dalkin took another chomp of his Smother Burger.

"Of course. There's even a specific banker."

"Dammit!" Dalkin looked pained.

"That upsets you?"

"No. I bit my tongue. Shit, it really hurts." Dalkin gulped cola and swigged it around. "Did you get . . . ?"

"No, she wouldn't say the banker's name–not yet anyway. She's a very cautious lady. I'm supposed to call her and report my progress. She said he'll give me the information as I need it."

"Hmm. You're supposed to call her from home?"

"No," said Squallace. "Public phones only."

"Do you think that rule applies to the women in Perth?"

"I'd be surprised if it didn't."

Dalkin nodded, satisfied. "You did good, Squallace." He dug into his pants pocket and produced an envelope containing twenty five hundred dollars in cash. "Treat yourself to something nice. Lo mein."

43

Fifteen special agents from the Federal Bureau of Investigation were milling inside and outside Hobby Lobby on Cerrilos Road in Santa Fe, New Mexico, when the artist strolled in. Earlier, the store's owner had phoned in a tip after seeing the Bureau's stat sheet, along with Disney's reward offer.

Federal agents waited patiently until the artist had selected seven tubes of oil paint and two brushes, and was standing at the cash register to pay.

"Freeze–FBI!" shouted one agent.

Four others pulled guns and aimed them at the artist.

The artist, surprised, slipped his right hand into his jacket.

"Don't move!" a second special agent hollered.

The artist began to pull his hand out of the jacket.

Shots from four pistols roared, heaving the shop with a decibel wave. A bucketful of lead took flight.

The artist folded, blood seeping from a dozen wounds.

Several agents huddled over his lifeless body.

"He was going for his gun, wasn't he?" said one.

"Yeah, I saw him. It's in his jacket."

The first agent reached into the bloodied garment to expose a hand clutching something. "Huh, what's this?"

It wasn't a gun. It was a white card that the artist held between thumb and forefinger. Upon it, these words were printed in bold:

I am a deaf mute. My name is Morton Drabowski. My address is . . . .

"Shit," said the FBI agent. "We're fucked."

44

JEFF DALKIN COULD HAVE ordered copies of Lucy Dengrove's itemized telephone bills from his shadowy information broker—a data-base digger named Chuck Schvantz. The going price was $1,895 for long-distance calls in any thirty-day period. But Dalkin decided against nickel-and-dime tactics. With serious expense money in the bank, he was prepared to spring for a ballistic approach.

Schvantz's computer hacker needed only Lucy Dengrove's e-mail call sign. And five grand in cash money. Then, equipped with a lap-top, modem, and public telephone, he would uncover her sign-on code, break into her computer and suck it dry. Everything would be left undisturbed. No fingerprints.

Illegal? Very.
Effective? As all hell.

In toto, Lucy Dengrove's word processing program contained sixty-four files. They ranged from her comical attempts at romantic poetry to bank checking account transactions to individual files on each of the women she had helped re-settle overseas. In a feeble stab at security, Dengrove had used numeric designations for files instead of actual names. Which meant Dalkin had to peruse them number by number until "Num-8" revealed the most vital details of Nancy Muro, "formerly known as Ellen Alouwahlia."

"Am I a smart sonofabitch or what?" Dalkin said aloud. He was alone in his room at the Olcott Hotel, to which he had decamped to escape the intrusion of two FBI special agents, shifting round-the-clock in his home, awaiting Willard Stukey's next call.

Dalkin's cell phone whistled. He had stopped using this phone—partly to keep it clear, but also to avoid FBI eavesdropping on non-Stukey calls. He flipped it open. "Yeah-what?"

"It's me," said Willard Stukey. "See the news?"

"Uh, what. . .?"

"The feds shot a deaf mute they thought was me. Strange it should happen out here."

"Out where?" said Dalkin. "Hold on, I'll put the TV on."

CNN was reporting a case of mistaken identity in the shooting death of a deaf mute by the FBI.

"Butt-wiping bargsters," cursed Dalkin.

"Anyhoo," said Stukey, "I've sent you two pictures by Federal Express. You should get them tomorrow. Sell them. See ya—bye."

"Hello? Hello?" Dalkin picked up his hotel phone and pounded R. James Cloverland's direct line.

"James Clover. . ." his secretary answered.

"Put him on. It's Dalkin."

Ten seconds later. "Jeff!"

"Don't *Jeff* me! What a crock of bogus shit you're pulling. You were supposed to wait for me to pinpoint Stukey's location! That was the plan! Lo mein!"

"Whose plan?"

"*My* plan, goddammit!"

"Jeff, you don't work for the Bureau."

"You're damn right I don't! Get those fucking goons out of my apartment!"

"You don't mean that, Jeff."

"The hell I don't. Floto! Lo mein! Tekka maki! Crab cakes! Wali of Swat!"

"You're not thinking straight, Jeff. If you're not in contact with Willard Stukey on our behalf, then you're aiding and abetting a wanted criminal. That's a very serious crime."

"Yeah, like, it's not a crime to gun down innocent deaf mutes?"

"Calm down, buddy. Let's start again. Hold a sec, my other line. . ."

Dalkin steamed.

"My guys tell me you just spoke to Stukey," Cloverland returned. "He sent you two pictures. I guess we're back to your plan. Okay?"

"Okay, my ass." Dalkin slammed the phone down.

Three minutes later, his cell phone whistled. "Yeah– what?"

"It's me," said Cloverland.

"You want to talk to me with those two intel-pukes listening in?"

"No," said Cloverland. "Call me back on another line."

"Fuck you." Dalkin clapped his cell phone shut and threw it across the room. He picked up the desk phone and touch-keyed another number. "Mark? It's me, Dalkin."

"Have you found my children yet?" demanded Mark Alouwahlia.

"Yeah, matter of fact I have," said Dalkin.

"Where?" The Indian's voice practically leapt through the earpiece, vibrating Dalkin's eardrum like a trampoline.

"That's exactly what I want to come see you about. Wali of Swat. Crab cakes. Tekka maki."

"You cannot tell me on the phone? I must know. Where are my children?"

"Slow down, pal," said Dalkin. "Like I said, we need to do this in person. Special considerations."

"What special considerations?"

"That's what we're going to talk about, face to face. I can grab the next Metroliner if you're free this evening."

"Of course, I make myself free," said Alouwahlia. "All I care is my children, where they are. If you know where, you should tell me."

"Yep, that's what I'm coming down to talk about," said Dalkin. "I can be at the Four Seasons at six o'clock."

Mark Alouwahlia was tapping his heel, seated upon a sofa in the Four Seasons' lounge, when Jeff Dalkin strode in. The Indian didn't rise, but anxiously shook Dalkin's hand from a rumped position.

Dalkin seated himself next to Alouwahlia on the sofa and leaned back, elbows butterflied behind his head—a study of self-assuredness with a half-smirk. Like Bruce Willis.

"Well?" Alouwahlia asked impatiently. "Where are my children?"

Dalkin nodded earnestly, and leaned forward. "I know exactly where they are. I have their new address."

"Where?" Alouwahlia glowered. This was a man who

did not like to be kept waiting.

"There's something I'd like to show you." Dalkin dug into a canvas brief bag and extracted a large envelope. From it he pulled an eight-by-twelve glossy color photograph. He held it up, facing Alouwahlia. "Is this your ex-wife?"

Alouwahlia clenched his jaw and looked at the bruised, swollen face. Two purple eyes and a fat, bloodied lip. "Where do you get this picture?" Anger flashed in the Americanized Indian's bulging eyes.

"I'm a very thorough investigator," said Dalkin. "Is this your ex-wife?"

Alouwahlia didn't answer.

"This is your ex-wife," Dalkin answered for him.

"This is not your business," said Alouwahlia.

"Not my business?" Dalkin flipped the photograph around to look at it. "It's my business to find her, so I should know what she looks like, right?"

"I ask you to find my children," said Alouwahlia.

"Did you do this to her?" asked Dalkin.

"Do what?"

Dalkin turned the picture so it faced Alouwahlia again. "*This.*"

"I tell you," whined Alouwahlia. "She is nymphomaniac. She disgraces herself. And me. She deserves this."

"I see." Dalkin slipped the photo back into the envelope. "Before we get into where your kids are, I just want to tell you something: If this woman were my sister, I'd kick your Wali of Swat butt from here to Bangalore and give you a vindaloo enema."

"How dare you speak like this!" Alouwahlia bellowed. "You work for me!"

"No." Dalkin shook his head. "I work for myself. Sometimes, if the money's real good, I undertake assignments from ass-wipes like you. And that's what we're going to talk about next: money." Dalkin paused. "I've just about fulfilled my side of the deal. I know where your children are, and I'm about to get to work proving it. But before I do, you need to deposit one million dollars, less my twenty grand advance, into an escrow account controlled by a neutral lawyer. Once the lawyer is satisfied that I have told you where your children are living, he will transfer the funds to my account."

Alouwahlia crossed his arms and narrowed his eyes. "You must tell me where my children are!"

"I don't have to do anything," said Dalkin. "But I'll tell you where your children are living once steps are taken to safeguard my reward."

Alouwahlia glared at Dalkin. Then he started screaming. "I pay you twenty thousand dollars! You must tell me where are my children!"

"That's funny," said Dalkin, calmly regarding the attention that the Indian's histrionics—and his own likeness to Bruce Willis—was creating among the patrons around them. "I could've sworn I just covered what needs to happen first."

Alouwahlia rose, bristling.

Assuming that this signaled the end of their discussion, Dalkin stood, too. Out the corner of his eye, he saw it coming.

Alouwahlia threw a punch.

Dalkin deflected the blow with his left wrist, then executed an upside-down karate chop—between the Indian's legs—his right thumb knuckle connecting with Alouwahlia's scrotum.

The Indian gasped and fell to his knees, trying to catch a breath.

"Let me know within forty-eight hours that you've created an escrow account with my reward," said Dalkin softly, leaning down. "Otherwise, I'll hire myself out to your ex-wife as her bodyguard. Lo mein."

The cocktail waitress that Alouwahlia had snapped his fingers at one week earlier swooned as Dalkin swaggered past.

45

"OUT! GET OUT!" Dalkin hollered at the FBI technicians in his home.

"But..."

"No buts. You're the butts. You've got five minutes to pick up all your garbage"–Dalkin motioned at the telephone tracking equipment and reel-to-reel tape recorder–"and get the hell out of my home. If you're still around in six minutes, first I'm gonna call the New York cops to arrest you for criminal trespass and second I'm gonna kick your ass."

Next morning at nine-forty-six, a knock on Dalkin's door.

He peered through the peephole, expecting a new shift of special agents to kick in the ass. It was a courier for Federal Express.

Dalkin opened.

"Mr. Jeff Dalkin? Sign here."

Dalkin signed, closed the door, tore open the parcel pack wrapping. Inside: two pictures, oil on board. One, a sunrise behind a low mountain range; the other, a bold sunset in fiery colors against a purple night, with adobe structures in the foreground.

Dalkin's landline phone rang.

"Yeah—what?" he answered.

"Calmed down yet?" said R. James Cloverland.

"Yeah, I'm real calm. Wali of Swat, Wali of Swat, crab cakes, tekka maki, lo mein."

"You sound calm."

"What do you want?"

"Why did you throw my men out?"

"They were getting on my nerves," said Dalkin. "How would you like two G-men hovering around you, calculating how many misdemeanors and felonies you're committing? And anyway, we're way beyond that now. Stukey's paintings arrived."

"Really?"

"Truly."

"Can we see them?"

"You can *buy* them. Five hundred grand each."

"C'mon, Jeff. We can't pay you a million dollars."

"Well, somebody better," said Dalkin. "There's an elusive million bucks—blow me—out there with my name on it. And I want it all, whether it's from an ugly Indian—curry-quaffing cunt-face—the Bureau—butt-wiping baloney-beaters—or Michael Ei . . . oh, shit . . . Ei . . . fuck . . . Ei-yi-yi-yi!" Dalkin sang like a Mexican mariachi who'd bitten into a burrito stuffed with chili peppers. "Or maybe I'll just sell them to the Museum of Modern Art. Yeah, I think I'll call that Mr. Fancypants—the curator, Sugarman. Unless *you* are offering some kind of reward for Stukey's capture?"

"We had a meeting about that," said Cloverland, "and decided we don't have to. Disney's reward is a big enough incentive for John Q. Citizen."

"That's just grand. John Q. Citizen can make two million dollars—blow me—but I'm the key to this thing and I can't make zip. I'm getting fucked by everyone. Lo mein."

"Maybe you should call Eisner and make a deal?"

"If I knew how to kiss ass, kiss ass, kiss ass . . . I'd still be at the Bureau—butt-wiping baloney-beating bottom-snorting bargsters. Bye." Dalkin disconnected Cloverland and phoned MoMA's curator.

"Oh, hello!" said Nathaniel Sugarman. "How are you?"

"Fine."

"I was just talking about you yesterday."

"Yeah?"

"About Tourette's syndrome."

"Great. Listen, I have two more Willard Stukey paintings."

"Do you now?"

"Yeah, here and now. I want to sell them. Lo mein. You interested?"

"We already have twenty on exhibition."

"Right, on loan. I'm offering you the chance to *own* a few."

"It's not as simple as that," said Sugarman. "We have a purchasing committee which sits monthly. Furthermore, our budget for this calendar year has already been allocated."

"Okay, then give me some advice," said Dalkin. "Who *would* want to buy these paintings?"

"Hmmm. I'd be very curious to see how they fare at auction," said Sugarman. "I'd recommend Sotheby's. You might give Anthony Thistle-Gizzard a tinkle. And feel free to mention my name."

As he touch-keyed Sotheby's, Dalkin wondered what kind of commission was in it for Sugarman. A minute later he had Anthony Thistle-Gizzard on the line. The upshot was this: Thistle-Gizzard was very interested, indeed, and could slot them into an auction three months hence.

"I want to sell them now," said Dalkin. "Today, this week."

Thistle-Gizzard was afraid it didn't work like that.

Frustrated, Dalkin stuffed the Stukey pictures under his bed mattress and zipped out to Starbucks on Lexington Avenue and Seventy-eighth Street.

Squallace. This was the name-slash-notion that popped into Dalkin's mind as caffeine from drip coffee stirred his brain cells. Olivia Squallace.

He, Dalkin, was disqualified from claiming Disney's reward for capturing Willard Stukey. But Olivia Squallace was very qualified. He dipped into his pocket for the cell phone, but it wasn't there. Just as well, he shrugged, the Bureau was probably tapping that line. Dalkin drained his paper cup of grounds and zipped to a street corner public phone.

"Hey, ain't you Bruce Willis?" said a hot dog vendor

"I'm late for a hot date with Nicole Kidman," said Dalkin, recognizing a tabloid tipster. "Dress for dinner," he spoke through the mouthpiece to Squallace. "I'm taking you to that frog place."

Over seventy-eight-dollar platters of frog legs sauteed in garlic butter and a two-hundred-dollar bottle of Opus

One in La Grenouille on Fifty-second Street, Jeff Dalkin laid out The Plan to Olivia Squallace: They would fly to Albuquerque, New Mexico, show Stukey's paintings to locals, figure out where he was painting, go there, surprise Stukey, and Squallace would execute a citizen's arrest.

At a nearby table, two undercover FBI special agents more accustomed to following UN diplomats, ate salads way over budget and watched Dalkin.

46

NEXT MORNING, DALKIN and Squallace shared a cab to Kennedy International Airport and checked in for United's 10:50 flight to Albuquerque.

Behind them, a new shift of undercover special agents quickly learned where the pair was headed and scrambled for tickets.

At the end of the gate ramp, Dalkin poked his head into the cabin. "This isn't a DC-nine, is it?"

"No, Mr. Willis," said a smiling female flight attendant. "This is a Boeing seven-thirty-seven."

Dalkin smirked. He and Squallace seated themselves and buckled up.

It was somewhere over Missouri, two hours into the flight, that the aircraft stopped humming.

In eerie silence, Dalkin and Squallace looked up from their pulp novels and exchanged a glance.

"If I didn't know better," whispered Dalkin, "I'd say both engines are down."

Squallace did not have a chance to reply. Her breath was taken when the plane lurched, then plunged.

Dalkin's stomach somersaulted from the G-force that pinned him deep into his seat.

When Squallace's breath returned, it emanated from her lungs with a squeal.

The jet continued to dive, nose straight down.

Passengers who could find their voice, let it rip; hand luggage spilled from overhead compartments and whizzed south through the cabin.

This couldn't be how it ends. That thought consumed Dalkin. He was more astounded than frightened. He simply couldn't comprehend that this could be the sum total of his life.

Twenty seconds into its plunge, an eternity to passengers, the jet's nose seemed to rise—the G-force decreased—and then it leveled out, just above a layer of cloud.

Engines hummed.

Shouts of horror evolved into cries of relief. Several passengers had been injured; others were in shock; flight attendants scurried to assist.

"This is Captain Riggs, your pilot," said a commanding voice over the intercom. "We experienced some engine trouble, but everything's back to normal now. Some of our passengers may need medical attention, so we're going to land in St. Louis in about fifteen minutes. I apologize for the inconvenience."

"Cool bastard," said Dalkin. "That does it. Seven-thirty-sevens are out. And DC-tens. And I think I'll add old seven-forty-sevens to the list, too. Wali of Swat, crab cakes, Floto, tekka maki, lo mein."

Squallace couldn't speak.

"Squallace, you okay? Lo mein."

Even with all her colourful make-up, Squallace was white as a fresh snowfall.

"A few seconds more..." she uttered, "and..."

A convoy of ambulances and fire engines, lights a-flashing, greeted the jet when it thumped onto a St. Louis runway, then taxied uneventufully to a gate. Captain Riggs announced that a new aircraft was standing by at a neighboring gate to carry on to Albuquerque, minus whoever needed medical care.

Dalkin and Squallace filed out; behind them, two pale-faced FBI special agents.

"Holy fucking Christ!" Dalkin mouthed off when he saw the new aircraft, which wasn't new at all, but a very, very old DC-nine. "First they put us on a plane renowned for falling out of the sky, and now they want to stick us on a DC-fucking-nine!"

Squallace regarded Dalkin bemusedly.

Dalkin dug his heels into the ramp at the cabin door, holding up people traffic behind him. "I'm not doing it, I'm not getting on, I'm not going, Wali of Swat, crab cakes, tekka maki, lo mein."

"What's the problem?" a male flight attendant asked cheerfully.

"This crappy old plane," shot Dalkin.

"It's quite all right," said the steward. "Bruce Willis?"

"It's quite all right?" echoed Dalkin. "You think it's quite all right to free-fall for a mile thinking you're about to be mutilated into a hundred-and-fifty pieces—and then be herded onto one of these, these ear-popping antiques? It's *not* quite all right, you dumb sonofabitch–blow me–I'm outta here." Dalkin turned to leave.

"Excuse me, Mr. Willis," said the flight attendant, "but do you have any checked luggage?"

Dalkin whipped around. "Yeah, three pieces between us." he motioned at Squallace. "And I'm *not* Bruce W-W-Willis. Lo mein."

"We can't take your luggage without you."

"Damn right. I want it back."

"I understand what you've been through," said the flight attendant earnestly. "It would be so much easier. . ."

"You and your airline don't understand shit!" Dalkin snapped. "I'm not stepping on a DC-fucking-nine you toady little pantload, and if you can't take my luggage without me –and you can't because it's a breach of security if you do– you can go fish it out, Sam." Dalkin picked up Sam's name from the plastic badge pinned to Sam's uniform. "Lo mein, goddammit!"

"I'll have a word with the pilot," said Sam.

"Have a word with the Easter Bunny if you want. I'm history." Dalkin whipped around and, with Squallace, squeezed past the passengers behind him, including two FBI special agents who exchanged puzzled glances. They, too, quickly decided not to board, an act noted by Dalkin.

"Hold on, Mr. Willis," the flight attendant called after Dalkin. "We need to know what your luggage looks like."

"Damn right you do," Dalkin hollered back. "I'll be at the nearest bar. Send someone to see me so's I can kick their ass, too."

While airline personnel rummaged around for luggage belonging to Jeff Dalkin and Olivia Squallace, the pair nursed hard liquor and eyed two special agents who had attempted, awkwardly, to blend into the airport milieu.

Dalkin rose and approached the two men, who had checked no luggage, but were sitting nearby, waiting, watching.

"You're burned, you stupid nosepicks," spat Dalkin. He strode past the startled spooks to a public phone and collect-called the assistant director of the FBI.

"Jeff, where are you?" asked Cloverland.

"Don't where-are-you me," growled Dalkin. "Your two nosepicks are right here watching, hoping I'll lead you Bureau butt-wiping bargsters to Willard Stukey."

"Isn't that where you're headed?"

"Maybe. But if I am, it's my collar, not yours. No, strike that, lo mein–it's Squallace's collar. Call 'em off. You'll get your man, but I need to handle this on my terms."

"Stukey's armed and dangerous," said Cloverland sternly.

"Don't cliché me," said Dalkin. His cell phone whistled.

"Now what," he muttered.

"What?" said Cloverland.

"Huh? Not you. You're over." Dalkin cradled the public receiver and flipped his mobile open. "Yeah–what?"

It was Mark Alouwahlia, the Wali of Swat's cousin, wanting to know where his children were living.

"We've already been through this," said Dalkin. "Did you open an escrow account?"

Alouwahlia had. He recited the details for Dalkin to

confirm himself. Dalkin did. Nine hundred and eighty thousand dollars had been deposited into a neutral account.

    Dalkin pocketed his phone, mind racing. "Pip, pip." He clapped his hands as he passed the two befuddled special agents, on his return to Squallace at the bar. "Where's our . . . ?"

    Squallace pointed to a pile of luggage behind her stool.

    "Excellent." Dalkin drained his gin and tonic. "Let's boogie."

    "Where now?" Squallace didn't really care at a thousand bucks a day and a new lease on life.

    "Australia."

    "Really?"

    "Truly. I need to lose those nosepicks." Dalkin threw a glance at the two watchers. "Oh, and we're back in business with that Indian–Wali of Swat, Wali of Swat, crab cakes, lo mein."

    Within fifteen minutes, Dalkin had it figured: TWA to Los Angeles; Quantas to Sydney, Australia; a connection to Perth.

47

SQUALLACE OPENED HER loins. Dalkin plugged his pecker deep into her palace of pleasure. He pounded. She panted.

"Oh, my God!" Squallace groaned.

"Wali of Swat, Wali of Swat, Floto, crab cakes, tekka maki, lo mein . . . mama!"

When Dalkin was spent, he rolled onto his back and studied the stained ceiling of their deluxe hotel room. Only one room had been available, thus the slumber party.

It wasn't that the pair were romantically inclined; simply that both needed a release after a brush with death and twenty hours on three jetliners to Perth.

The two FBI special agents had been left behind in Los Angeles, dumbfoundedly scratching their nuts. They had not brought passports; had not counted on trans-Pacific travel.

After a caffeine infusion, Squallace set out on a Dalkin-financed shopping spree—clothes and accessories—and

Dalkin found an electronics shop. He equipped himself with a 35mm Nikon camera, a telephoto lens and a couple rolls of Kodak color film. He also picked up a detailed, street-indexed map book of Perth. And finally, through the concierge, he arranged for a rental car to be delivered to the hotel.

About two p.m., Dalkin and Squallace set off in search of Slater Street, in the northwest suburbs. After a few false turns, they found their destination: 114 Slater Street, home to Mrs. Ellen Alouwahlia, alias Nancy Muro, and her children.

This being a weekday, Dalkin's expectation was to witness, photographically, a return home from school. The reality was better: both children were at play on the front lawn, beneath Australian sunshine, outside their modest ranch house.

Dalkin drove past, circled, passed again and stopped three houses away.

Not fifteen minutes later, Nancy Muro appeared at the front door with lemonade for her kids. It was picture perfect. Literally.

"They look so happy," Squallace commented.

Dalkin was silent for a moment. "So?"

"So. I'm just saying they look so happy together."

"Spell it out, Squallace."

"Are you sure you want to. . . ?"

"They'll be fine," snapped Dalkin. "It'll be impossible to extradite them. Lo mein."

"What if he flies over here and shoots her?"

Dalkin shrugged. He hadn't considered that possibility. "It's not my problem."

Squallace lowered her camera. "Maybe we should warn her."
Dalkin squinted at Squallace. "Have you lost your marbles? It must be jet lag. Tekka maki. Lo mein. I'm on the verge of becoming a millionaire, for chrissakes!"
"It might be blood money."
Dalkin ignored her. "Take a coupla shots of the whole block," he instructed, "and the street sign."
"If you make a million out of this, you could afford to give her some of it to escape." Squallace clicked the shutter release button several times, stopped, looked at him. "So?"
"So what? If we warn her and she splits, that goddamn Indian will sue me for his money back. No. Wali of Swat. Lo mein."
"But you saw what he did to her," Squallace pushed. "That picture."
"They're not married anymore. She'll get a restraining order."
"What if he shows up here with a gun?"
"Shit, Squallace, you're letting your female emotions interfere with this assignment. She'll be all right. Drop it."

There was no point lingering in Perth. Dalkin had a million reasons—in dollars—awaiting him. And Willard Stukey was waiting, too, along with another potential two mil. So off he and Squallace flew, Quantas to Sydney, Sydney to LA, where Dalkin went to work on a public phone, mobilizing Mark Alouwahlia and the escrow lawyer, arranging for a rendezvous the next day in Philadelphia.

48

"BRUCE WILLIS?" This was the escrow lawyer, Matthew Hopkins, as Dalkin entered the conference room of Hopkins & Horn, where he and Alouwahlia were waiting.

"I'm not Bruce W-W-Willis. Name's Jeff Dalkin." Dalkin shook the lawyer's outstretched hand. "Lo mein."

"You look exactly like Bruce Willis," Hopkins marveled, eyes riveted on Dalkin.

"Yeah, right." Dalkin smirked, just like Bruce Willis, and sat down facing Mark Alouwahlia, who had not stood, but nodded once, unsmiling, in acknowledgement.

"Hi, Mark!–butt-faced bootlick from Bangalore–sorry, Tourette's, I saw your children."

Alouwahlia scowled. "Where are my children?" he demanded.

"I'm planning to tell you, once we reconfirm the financial arrangements." Dalkin turned to Hopkins, who had seated himself at the end of the long conference table, between the two men. "Okay, Matt, I will supply the address of Mark's ex-wife and children–current as of two days ago, with no reason to think it has changed—along with photographic evidence that I personally saw them at that address. You will then release nine hundred and eighty thousand dollars, a wire transfer to my account."

"Minus my escrow service fee," said Hopkins.

"How much?"

"One percent."

"Fuck me," said Dalkin. "That's an easy ten grand."

Hopkins pushed a two-page letter across the shiny mohagany surface to Dalkin. "All I need is your signature and social security number."

Dalkin signed, socialed, then plucked an index card from his pocket. "Here are my banking details." He handed the card to Hopkins. "I expect your wire today."

"I'll phone the bank personally," said Hopkins.

"Good." Dalkin unzipped a leather folio and produced a packet of five-by-seven glossy color photographs. He spread them across the table like a deck of cards.

"Your children"—he looked Alouwahlia in the eye—"are in Perth, Australia. Specifically, at one-one-four Slater Street. Here are pictures of the street, their house, your children and your ex-wife. She now calls herself Nancy Muro."

Alouwahlia grabbed at the pictures and looked at them three at a time, hands trembling. When he got to his ex-wife with lemonade on the sunny doorstep, the Indian's eyes turned to daggers. "The bitch," he hissed, then spit on the image. "I kill her for this," he whispered.

Hopkins, lawyer that he was, pretended not to hear.

"Are we done?" Dalkin looked at at Hopkins.

Hopkins looked to Alouwahlia for confirmation.

"How do we know this is real?" whined Alouwahlia.

"I'm glad you asked that," said Dalkin. "As you can see, the photos are date-coded." Dalkin reached into his folio. "Here are my round-trip ticket stubs to Perth. Here is the computer file kept on your ex-wife by a woman who helped her escape. Any reasonable man would see this is real."

Hopkins peered over a pair of reading glasses at Alouwahlia. "I'm satisfied."

"Good." Dalkin turned to Alouwahlia. "Now, just so we understand each other, there's something you should know: If anything physical happens to this woman, I'm going to cut your pecker off and shove it down your throat. Lo mein."

Alouwahlia glared at Dalkin. "Who do you think you are, talking like this to me?" the Indian bellowed. "Did she sleep with you, too?"

Dalkin stood and winked. "Helluva lay."

Hopkins scrambled to his feet and guided Dalkin by the elbow to the door while Alouwahlia grunted and hissed incoherently.

49

Early that evening, after confirmation of the lawyer's wire transfer, Jeff Dalkin direct-dialed Perth, Australia.

A child answered.

"Is your mom there?" asked Dalkin.

The child did not answer, but scampered off. "Mommy, mommy. It's a *man*."

Thirty seconds passed. "Hello?" It was a reluctant hello.

"Nancy?" said Dalkin.

"Who is this?" said the former Mrs. Alouwahlia.

"Never mind who I am. Lo mein. Shit."

"What?"

"Your husband–boot-lick from Bangalore, dammit!– he knows where you are," Dalkin blurted, wishing to get this over with. The biggest problem with Tourette's was that it left footprints as his signature tune.

Silence.

"I'm serious," said Dalkin.

"I don't know what you mean," said Nancy Muro, her voice trembling.

"Listen to me," said Dalkin. "Mark knows. This isn't a prank. He found out a few hours ago."

"How?"

"How's not important. He knows. You've got at least twenty-four hours before he could turn up. Lo mein."

"Oh my God. He's coming here?"

"It's possible," said Dalkin. "That's why I'm calling. Get out of there. Go somewhere else. Floto, crab cakes. Good luck." Dalkin put down the public phone at Penn Station. He'd done the right thing. The rest was up to her.

Later, back home, Dalkin sat with a desk calculator and a pad of paper.

The first twenty grand was gone. He owed Squallace six grand–doubled to twelve, a bonus. And, oh shit, Harvey Kimbach would be looking for his ten percent. That left $858,200. Then Dalkin calculated state and federal income tax. Bottom line, he'd made $514,920. He shook his head, disgusted. How did anybody get to be a millionaire–blow me–anyway?

Then his jet-lag-addled mind rememembered: Willard Stukey. Two paintings, Michael Aye-yi-yi-Eisner's reward. That elusive one million–after expenses, commissions, tax –it was out there, somewhere. . . .

50

WILLARD STUKEY WAS growing restless. CNN and the networks had cut their Mickey Murder Manhunt coverage to half what it had been. Even with this notoriety and a comparison to van Gogh at MoMA and inside the *New York Times*, he still hadn't made the cover of *Time* magazine. He should have demanded *that* along with his original conditions.

The artist had already changed motels twice in Santa Fe. And, inspiration waning, he was weary of desert and mountain lanscapes. Maybe it was time to re-charge with the stratospheric high that came only from a live art exhibition?

But money was running out. Stukey needed a cash infusion. What was that danged agent doing? Stukey had called three times, no answer. Had the bastard sold his two pictures and fled to retirement on the Riviera? Stukey smoldered. Where was the public phone in this dive?

Dalkin's cell phone whistled and startled him from a

jet lag-induced trance at his desk. "Yeah—what?" he answered.

"This is Willard Stukey," said the artist. "Where've you been?"

"Australia."

"Oh." Stukey was stumped. "To sell my paintings?"

"You *are* a self-absorbed sonofabitch," snapped Dalkin. "I went to scout out other artists."

"Oh. What about *my* paintings?"

"What about them?"

"Did they arrive?"

"Yeah."

"Did you sell 'em?"

"Not yet. That fancy-pants curator at MoMA suggested we auction them at Sotheby's. So I called Sotheby's—some limey bastard—and he said they'll put them in a sale three months from now."

"Fuck that," Stukey whined. "I need money. Just walk 'em over to some of those snotty galleries on Fifty-seventh Street. Sell 'em cheap if you have to. I've got plenty more."

"Okay, I'll get on it in the morning. Where can I reach you?"

"I'll call you tomorrow, same time, see ya—bye."

Standing next to the public phone as New Mexico's flourescent pink sunset faded to purple, Stukey considered his next move. Then he flipped through his pocket notebook for a number he had not rung in a while. He pre-fixed it with a zero and made it collect.

"Willard?" Hugh Scrupula, producer of Breaking News at CNN, could hardly believe it.

"Yeah, it's me."

"Where are you now?"

"Out here, Hugh. I've been painting. But I'm ready to strike again."

"Oh, no–shit... don't..." Scrupula envisaged Stukey about to launch another over-the-phone shooting spree.

"Put me on TV," said Stukey. "I want to say something."

"I can't, Willard."

"Why the hell not?"

"Orders from the president."

"Of the United States?"

"No. The president of CNN."

"That's really bogus. I'm a famous artist now," Stukey ranted. "They're comparing me to van Gogh. But I'm better than that nutcase Dutchman."

"But–my God–you've killed fifty people!"

"Christ, why does everybody keep worrying about *that?* It won't mean a thing in a hundred years, Hugh. Really. My art will be in museums. There'll be fifty books about me, and more written every decade. *That's* what matters. Only art endures. People are unripened wormmeat."

"I'm not putting you on, Willard."

"Fine. Then I'll go kill Donald Duck."

"Don't do it, Willard."

"I will."

"It won't prove anything," said Scrupula. "You're already famous."

"Yeah, but I bet you'll put me back on TV after I murder Donald Duck."

"No. Murdering Donald Duck won't change our policy."

"Then I'll call that tall guy with the microphone up his ass."

"Who?"

"You know," said Stukey. "The one on ABC."

"Peter Jennings?"

"Yeah, Jennings. He'll put me on."

"No, Willard. ABC is owned by Capital Cities, which is owned by Disney." Scrupula paused. "I've got a better idea. I could get you on TV with an in-person interview."

"In person?"

"Right," said Scrupula. "Face to face."

"Hmmm. That means we'd have to meet."

"Right."

"I don't know, Hugh. That sounds like it could be a definite hindrance to my freedom. I'll think about it some. I like CNN. It goes around the world. They should know about me in Germany and Japan. Teach those German post-war expressionists a lesson in art. Sleds. What a crock. See ya–bye."

51

THE WALLY FINDLAY GALLERY looked the right sort of place. Dalkin ducked into this swanky art gallery on Fifty-seventh Street with a small package tucked beneath his arm.

"Mr. Willis?" A well-groomed thirty-something male in a decent suit appeared from an office. "I didn't know you were a collector." He winked. "We have many of your colleagues in Hollywood as clients. Is that how you heard of us?"

Dalkin shook his head, smirking. "I'm here to sell, not to collect. Lo mein."

"Oh?" The salesman's enthusiasm was short-lived.

"I have two paintings by Willard Stukey," Dalkin announced.

"The Mickey murderer?"

"Bingo. Wali of Swat, Wali of Swat, tekka maki, crab cakes, lo mein." Dalkin unwrapped the first picture and held it out. "Hang it under a spot," he suggested.

The salesman did this. His eyes widened. "It . . . it's awesome." In truth, it was an astonishing explosion of color:

blood reds, inferno oranges—as if the sun, in setting, had collided with earth.

Dalkin unwrapped the second painting. Its boldness was equally breathtaking.

"You really want to sell these?" asked the salesmen.

"Yep."

"Where did you get them?"

"From the artist," said Dalkin.

"They're *good*."

"Yeah. Sotheby's wants to auction them. But I'm looking for a quick fix."

"I see. I'd like to discuss this with Mr. Findlay. Do you mind waiting a few minutes?"

"Go ahead. Lo mein."

Dalkin waited. The salesman returned five minutes later.

"We'd be delighted," he said, "to take these paintings on consignment. We have several clients who might be interested in pur—"

"Consignment?"

"Yes. We try to sell them for you."

"No, no. We're not communicating," said Dalkin. "I want to sell them to *you*. I can let you have them way below what they'd fetch at Sotheby's. You wait out a sale and make a big profit. I need the cash now."

"I don't think. . . ."

"It's not a thinking matter," said Dalkin. "You either want to buy them, or I go to the next gallery."

"I see." The salesman was less friendly now. "Allow me to advise Mr. Findlay."

"Yeah, advise Mr. Findlay—fucking fancypants from

faggotville—no, I . . . never mind." Explaining Tourette's was mostly a time-waster.

Five minutes later, Dalkin's impatience was replaced with anxiety, intensified by the distant ululating of a siren, growing louder.

"Hello?" Dalkin called out.

No one answered.

The siren drew nearer.

Dalkin plucked his pictures from the wall and made for the door. It was locked. Now Dalkin realized he'd been double-crossed because he wouldn't give up the paintings on consignment. He looked around for inspiration, found it in a desk chair, which he hurled it through the gallery's front display window.

Alarm bells chimed.

Dalkin manuevred himself through jagged glass and surprised passersby as he jumped to the sidewalk.

"Bruce Willis?!" said one. "Are you shooting a movie?"

"Lo mein," said Dalkin. He straightened himself and, with a police cruiser barreling down a block away, scooted across Fifty-seventh Street shouting "pizza-puke-and-poops," onto Madison Avenue, down Fifty-sixth to Fifth Avenue, and into a taxi stopped at a red light. "Soup Burg, Madison and Seventy-third," he instructed. "Crinkum-crankum, pop-a-nut."

52

C NN HAD IT ON THE AIR by the time Dalkin got home, after devouring a Smother Burger Deluxe.

"A strange new twist in the Mickey Murder Manhunt," intoned a Breaking News correspondent standing on Fifty-seventh Street. "A short while ago, movie star Bruce Willis appeared in the art gallery behind me and tried to sell two paintings believed to have been painted by Willard Stukey. It is thought that Willis is in contact with the mass murderer. When police were called, Willis broke the gallery's front window and fled the scene on foot. Police sources tell CNN that they have issued a warrant for the actor's arrest on charges of aiding and abetting."

53

W ILLARD STUKEY TELEPHONED Dalkin on schedule.
"You're punctual for an artist," said Dalkin.
"What's going on?" Stukey sounded like his blood pressure was up. "Did you sell my paintings to Bruce Willis?"
"No, no. Here's what I've decided to do," said Dalkin. "*I'm* going to buy your paintings. Or at least make a down payment on them. How much do you need?"
"Fifty thousand?"
"Are you asking me?"
"No," said Stukey. "I want fifty thousand. Cash money."
"Done. Lo mein. You want me to Western Union it to you?" Dalkin knew he wouldn't.
"I want you to *bring* it to me."
"Sure." Dalkin was low-key, not wishing to show enthusiasm. "I could do that. What exactly do you have in mind?"
Stukey laid it out.

54

THE WAY DALKIN figured it—after forty minutes' figuring—New York's finest would probably discover that it was he who was peddling Willard Stukey's paintings for cash, not Bruce Willis. It was this need for an insurance policy against arrest for complicity that compelled Dalkin to pick up his phone and dial R. James Cloverland's home number.

"Ah, Jeff Dalkin," said a cocky Cloverland. He had Dalkin by the balls and both men knew it. "Of all the people in the world, Bruce Willis had to have *you* as a double. And the poor guy—can you imagine, he makes twenty million a movie and I'm calling him a poor guy? This poor guy blames all the trouble you cause him, all the time, on the tabloid press."

"Tell the cops—cop-a-cherry cunt-hounds. Set 'em straight," said Dalkin. "I'm not an accomplice. You know that. I'm trying to catch that sonofabitch."

"Now it doesn't *look* that way, does it?" Cloverland was enjoying this. "After all, you've refused to cooperate with law enforcement and you flew all the way to Australia just to lose my agents."

"You're taking that personally, Jim. I had *business* in Australia."

"Oh, I forgot. You've been helping men find the ex-wives they once brutalized. It might interest you that the New York City cops have your fingerprints on the chair you threw out that window. At first they weren't going to bother dusting it, because they were convinced it was Bruce Willis they wanted. But Bruce has a good alibi. He's doing a Planet Hollywood opening in Addis Abbaba, Ethiopia. Two thousand witnesses. So now they think someone was wearing a Bruce Willis mask and they've sent the chair to our forensics lab in Quantico."

"Listen, Jim, I just heard from Stukey. He wants to meet. He thinks I have money for him. Let's catch him together, you and me, in person, just like when we were special agents. I'll cuff, you Miranda."

"Why do I get the feeling this isn't a good faith offer?"

"You've got me groveling," said Dalkin. "You want me to kiss your feet, too?"

"You bet," said Cloverland. "I'm trying to make the most of a humbled Dalkin."

"You can joke, but I'm catching this guy with or without you," said Dalkin. "My only condition is that we use a Bureau–butt-wiping bargsters from baloneyville–one of your jets. I'm sick of dodging DC-nines and seven-thirty-sevens."

"Eisner spoiled you."

"What's new with that bastard anyway?"

"Who?"

"The joker you just mentioned."

"Who?"

"You know, Michael Ei . . . Ei . . . Ei . . . Aye-yi-yi-yi." Dalkin sang like a Mexican mariachi who'd just had his pecker cut off by a jealous lover.

"I know who you mean," said Cloverland. "I just wanted to hear you sing."

"Bastard. It ought to be a federal crime to make fun of a disbility like mine."

"Don't worry, they're working on it," said Cloverland. "We already have a workshop on dealing with lunatics, uh, the mentally challenged. Anyway, since you asked, Eisner is so mad at our director he can't pee straight."

"Him or the director?"

"Who?"

"Quit fucking with me, goddammit!"

"Eisner's pissed because Stukey's still out there. People are so scared, they won't even take their kids to see animated Disney movies." Cloverland paused. "All right, I'll requisition a jet. Where are we going?"

"South," replied Dalkin. "Can you pick me up at LaGuardia?"

"No chance. Shuttle your butt down to DC."

55

WILLARD STUKEY DID NOT like the clerk's attitude as he checked out of a Santa Fe motel. Part of the artist wanted to blow this snotty punk away with a Hechler & Koch MPSKA4 9mm machine pistol. Unfortunately, a live art exhibition at this juncture would only complicate matters. So Stukey reluctantly refrained.

Stukey tried to re-negotiate what he owed for five nights, but this punk refused to discount their price.

"You want me to starve?" asked Stukey. In truth, he was already hungry. Hungry for burgoo.

The clerk shrugged indifferently, and even charged a half-day rate for a dusk checkout.

"Where's the bus station?" demanded Stukey. "You want to charge me for information, too?"

The clerk pointed, his eyes affixed to a *Roseanne* re-run on a grimy black-and-white TV set.

56

Two minutes after landing at Reagan-National Airport, Dalkin's cell phone whistled. "Yeah—what?"
"Mr. Dalkin?"
"I said yeah."
"Please hold for Matthew Hopkins."
"Shit." Dalkin listened to static as he climbed into a taxi.
"We have a problem," Hopkins opened, no greeting.
"We?"
"Mr. Alouwahlia is in Australia."
"Already?"
"He went to the address you gave him with a representative from the U.S. Mission in Perth." Static danced around the lawyer's words. "His wife and children aren't there."
"Maybe they took a vacation."
"The house is empty."
"Empty? What do you mean empty?"
"There's nothing in it," said Hopkins. "No furniture,

nothing. Mr. Alouwahlia is very unhappy. He thinks he's been conned. He says he's going to file a complaint against you—and me, too—for fraud."

"Let's hope they put the F . . . F . . . fucked-up fatheads farting in a frenzy—FBI, said it, whew! Let's hope they put them on it."

"Why?"

"I can't hear you, you're breaking. . ." Dalkin switched off the phone.

57

Half asleep, Stukey gazed out the bus window as dawn broke over the city of Houston, Texas. Soon the large vehicle rumbled to a final, smelly stop. The artist disembarked, groggy, disheveled, and–down to his last fifty bucks–bought another bus ticket.

58

"I COULDN'T GET A JET," said Cloverland, reaching for his coat as Dalkin walked into the assistant FBI director's office.

"No jet?" Dalkin was agitated.

"No. They gave me a helicopter."

Dalkin stiffened. "Are you nuts? I'm not flying in a helicopter–Hershey squirt."

"They're perfectly safe."

"The hell they are." Dalkin twisted his head left and right. "I'm not getting in a helicopter. Hershey squirt, crab cakes, tekka maki, lo mein."

"For chrissakes, you sound like a Chesapeake-Japanese-Chinese waiter."

"I'm can't believe you're still making fun of my Tourette's. Wali of Swat, Wali of Swat."

"I can't believe you won't fly in a helicopter."

Dalkin shook his head violently. "No way, no way, no way..."

"Okay I'll cancel it," said Cloverland. "We'll fly commercial."

"No DC-nines, no seven-thirty-sevens, no . . ."

"Is this part of Tourette's?" Cloverland shook his head in disbelief.

"No. This is part of diving a mile, nose first, with a hundred and forty people screaming their fucking heads off."

59

Looking as if he'd slept in his suit on a bus, Willard Stukey arrived late morning at the downtown Atlanta office building. He swaggered to a CNN checkpoint manned by two uniformed security guards.

"I'm here to see Hugh Scrupula," Stukey announced.

The African-American guard, seated on a stool behind a podium-style desk, looked Stukey up and down. The artist's stained white shirt was open at the collar, no tie, and he sported a three-day growth, face and scalp, that resembled fungi. "Is he expecting you?"

"Sorta." Stukey shuffled his feet.

With some trepidation, the guard consulted a three-ring binder that alphabetized employees names and linked them to extension numbers. He touch-keyed three digits on his phone, and eyed Stukey. "What's your name?"

"Willard."

"Mr. Scrupula?" the guard spoke into his phone. "I have a Mr. Willard here to see you." The guard listened. "Uh-huh." He held the phone out to Stukey. "He wants to talk to you."

Stukey accepted the phone. "Hugh?"

"Willard? You're... *downstairs?*" Scrupula's voice was two octaves higher than usual.

"Yup."

"Wha... what do you want?"

"No, Hugh," Stukey spoke softly. "It's what *you* want."

"Excuse me?"

"You said you want to interview me, face to face. Remember? Here I am, downstairs. So let's get it on, guy."

"I, uh, gosh, I don't know. Do you have a gun?"

"Of course," said Stukey.

"You can't come up here!"

"The hell I can't. I came all the way here because you said you'd put me on TV as long as it was face-to-face, and now you're saying I can't come up and do it? That's a crock of shit, Hugh. I'm coming up." Stukey cradled the phone and looked from guard to guard. "He wants me to go up."

One guard shook his head. "I don't think that's what the man said."

"No? Well, I'm going." Stukey reached into his jacket. "Which one of you boys is gonna show me the way?"

"Look here, Mr. Willard..."

"No, you lookey here." Stukey pulled out his Hechler & Koch MPSKA4 9mm machine pistol and waved it at both men. "See? This is what you call a skeleton key–it gets you wherever you want to go. And I'm going up. Who's taking me?"

Both guards remained silent, transfixed upon Stukey's cold hard steel.

To speed up the proceedings, the artist discharged a single shot into one guard's leg. Blood seeped from his wound as he fell to the linoleum floor, bending his knee, holding his leg. "He shot me! Sweet Jesus, it hurts!"

Stukey pierced the other guard's frightened eyes with his own. "Your leg's next," said Stukey, "unless you're ready to take me up."

"No, no, don't shoot. This way." The guard backed up to the elevator bank behind his checkpoint.

Stukey followed him into an elevator.

"Which floor?" The guard glared at Stukey.

"How the hell do I know? Take me to the goddamn newsroom."

Hugh Scrupula dived onto his phone and tapped nine-one-one. An operator answered.

"This is Hugh Scrupula of CNN," said Scrupula, trying to remain calm. "Send police, ambulances, to our headquarters immediately."

"Is this an emergency?" asked the emergency operator.

"Of course it is!"

"What is the nature of your emergency?"

"Willard Stukey is here!" Scrupula shouted.

"Who?"

"C'mon, you must be the only person in America who doesn't know who Willard Stukey is. A mass murderer is in our building. Hurry!"

"What's your address, sir?"

"CNN. Everyone in Atlanta knows where we are. The police will know."

"Sir, I need you to tell me your address."

"One CNN Center!" Scrupula hollered.

Stukey tapped his right foot as the elevator ascended. It stopped. The doors opened.

"This our floor?" asked Stukey.

"Uh-uh," the security guard shook his head.

"Going up?" asked a man poised to step in.

"*We* are." Stukey pointed his gun. "You're not."

Scrupula burst out of his office in shirtsleeves. "Evacuate the newsroom!" he erupted. "Everyone out!"

A producer seated nearby cupped a phone. "Not another bomb scare, Hugh?"

"W-W-W-Willard Stukey!" Scrupula stammered, face drained of color. "He's on his way up!"

Producers and correspondents scrambled. The buzz fell into a hush as Willard Stukey strolled into the newsroom, machine pistol in hand. The collective news-shapers gawked at him.

"Anyone know where I can find Hugh Scrupula?" Stukey filled the silence, normal in voice, if not in appearance.

"I'm here." Scrupula stepped forward.

"Ah, the face behind the voice." Stukey smiled.

"Indeed." Scrupula planted himself six feet in front of Stukey as if to shield the newsroom.

A cacophony of wailing sirens could be heard in the distance.

"That's not for us, is it, Hugh?" asked Stukey.

Scrupula nodded. "Of course it is."

"That's kinda funny," said Stukey, grinnning.

"Funny?"

"Yeah. Usually CNN *goes* to war zones. Now the war

zone is coming to *you*. Who-eee! I'm an artist. I like irony."

Scrupula did not reply, remaining stern-faced as the circles of sweat beneath the armpits of his white shirt continued to spread.

"Okay," said Stukey. "Let's go *live*. Isn't that what you say?"

"Live?"

"Yeah. This *is* CNN, isn't it. This *is* news, isn't it? Let's get it on, guy."

Scrupula remained immobile.

"Do I have to *shoot* someone to make this newsworthy enough to go live?" Stukey waved his gun. "C'mon, guy—this is a seige. You're all hostages. It's not the way I wanted my interview to be, but, hey, whatever it takes."

60

"WHAT THE. . . ?" Dalkin glanced at a TV set hanging from the ceiling of an Atlanta airport bar as he strode past, then whirled around mid-stride. "It's Willard Stukey!"

"Where?" Cloverland froze, expecting an in-person Stukey.

With Cloverland in full pursuit behind him, Dalkin beat a path to the bar. "What's going on?"

"The Mickey murderer," said a suited, corpulent man stooled at the bar sipping from a frosted mug of beer. "He's taken over CNN."

"Was that *The Plan?*" Cloverland's sarcasm was lost on Dalkin.

"Right city, new twist. C'mon, let's go. Pop-a-nut."

"Hey," called the beer drinker, "aren't you Bruce Willis?"

61

WILLARD STUKEY WAS telling the world–live on CNN –his theory about art prevailing over the lives of men when the first police on the scene burst out of an elevator and entered the newsroom.

The artist calmly raised the Hechler & Koch MPSKA4 9mm machine pistol that rested upon his lap and fired several rounds at them.

The police retreated.

CNN's Stukey-appointed interviewer, Lou Waters, who had ducked beneath his anchor desk, re-seated himself and rubbed his ears. "What is it you want?" he beseeched Stukey.

"You know what I really want more than anything?" said Stukey.

"Please tell us," said Waters.

"I want a bowl of burgoo." Stukey alternated between looking at Lou, then at the camera, trying to act like Chevy Chase, the B-movie comic. "That's what I want, a bowl of good ol' Kentucky burgoo."

The anchor was uncomprehending. "Is that supposed to be a metaphor for something?"

"A what?" Stukey looked at Waters like he was nuts. "I just want a bowl of burgoo, you idiot. I've had my say. Now I want burgoo."

"Pardon me for asking," said Waters, "but what is a burgoo?"

Stukey grinned. "A famous newsman like you, been around the world 'n' all, and you don't even know burgoo? If that don't beat all. It's squirrel brain stew, dummy!"

The anchor's phone rang.

"May I answer that?" he asked Stukey.

"Go right ahead, Lou. But I bet it's for me." Stukey winked at the camera.

The anchor answered, listened. "It's for you," he said.

"Told you. This is *my* show, not yours, see?" Stukey put the phone to his ear and looked directly into the camera lens. "Joe's Pizza." He paused. "Just kidding!"

"This is Lieutenant Kyle Pickford," said a soothing voice. "I'm a hostage negotiator with the Atlanta Police Department. What's the situation in there, Willard?"

"Hi, Kyle, the rest of the world's way ahead of you on this one, guy. Just tune your TV to CNN."

"What do you want?" Pickford demanded.

"See what I mean?" said Stukey. "You've got some catching up to do, guy. I was just saying on live TV that what I really want just now is a bowl of burgoo."

"A what?"

"Jesus Christ!"

"Don't get upset," Pickford back-pedaled.

"I'm cool," said Stukey. "I just want a dang bowl of burgoo, which anyone with an ounce of sense knows is squirrel brain stew. Is that so goddamn difficult?"

"Okay, calm down. We'll try to get you a bowl of burgoo," said Lieutenant Pickford. "Anything else?"

"Yeah, as long as you're asking. I'd like an apology from Mr. Floto."

"Who?"

"Mr. Floto. My art teacher from high school. That sonofabitch was on TV bad-mouthing me. I want to hear what he has to say now that they're comparing my work to van-fucking-Gogh. That's what I want—a public apology from Mr. Floto."

"Uh, okay, I'll check that out."

"Check it out? Listen, Kyle, you're gonna need to get better informed if we're gonna talk some. Call me back when you've got my burgoo. See ya—bye." Stukey plunked the phone down. "I can see why you guys like to do this," Stukey said to Lou Waters. "It's fun. Do you think Saddam Hussein is watching?"

Waters shrugged. "He's been known to tune in."

"If you're watching right now, Saddam," said Stukey, "you can suck my paintbrush. You know what I hate most about Saddam?" Stukey spoke to Waters as if the pair were engaged in local news happy talk. "The only thing them artists are allowed to paint over there in I-raq are portraits of that grinning son-of-a-whore. In fifty years all those paintings will be burned. And damn right, too."

The phone rang.

"It's probably for you," said Waters, loosening his tie.

Stukey picked it up. "Hello?"

"This is Kyle Pickford . . ."

"You again?" Stukey mugged for the camera.

"Yes, I . . ."

"Did you order up my burgoo?"

"Working on it," said Pickford. "What I'd like you to do, Willard, is show some good faith by releasing your hostages."

"You think just because I'm a right-brain kinda guy that I'm totally nuts?" said Stukey. "I don't owe you no good faith."

"If I'm going to give you something, I need something in return."

"Okay, I'll draw you a picture." Stukey looked at Lou Waters. "You got a pen?"

The anchor dipped into his inside coat pocket for a pen.

"No," said Pickford. "I'm sure your pictures are nice, but–"

"*Nice?* You're sure my pictures are *nice?* You're probably the kind of guy who buys those mass-produced oil paintings of forests and streams on those cable TV stuff-for-sale shows for eighty-nine dollars. *Nice?* Fuck you. Don't patronize *me*, Kyle."

"No, I didn't mean. . ."

"You need a trade? Here's my trade. You give me what I ask for and I won't kill anyone."

"Okay, Willard, take it easy. We don't want anyone to get hurt."

"Except *me*," said Stukey.

"We're working on what you want . . ."

"Good," said Stukey. "Call me when you got my burgoo."

"Don't hang up!"

"I'm in the middle of a live broadcast to the world," said Stukey, "and you keep interrupting me. Have you found

Mr. Floto yet?"

"Uh . . . no."

"Well why don't you spend your time rounding up my burgoo and that fraudulent art teacher-who's-really-a-jerk-off Mr. Floto and then we'll have something to jawbone about."

"But . . ."

"See ya–bye." Stukey hung up and turned to Lou Waters. "Where were we, Lou?"

"Excuse me?"

"Oh, I remember," said Stukey. "Saddam Hussein. Does he really think that his ugly face is art? His own people should blow him away for littering Baghdad with so many portraits of himself. It's not like any of those portraits express any *truth* about him." Stukey put pen to paper and sketched. "Here." He held up his sketch of an anus for the camera. "I did this in fifteen seconds and it says more about Saddam Hussein than those larger-'n-life portraits he hangs everywhere."

The phone rang.

"I'm not answering it," said Stukey.

"May I?" asked Waters.

"Suit yourself. But make it quick. It'll be hard to talk to the world if you're babbling next to me."

Lou Waters answered, listened, stiffened. "He wants to talk to you."

"Who, Saddam Hussein?" Stukey winked at the camera.

"No."

"Well, I'm not talking to Kyle unless he has my burgoo."

"It's not the police," said Waters.

"Then who?"

"Ted Turner."

"Who?"

"Our owner."

"*Our* owner?" said Stukey. "*I* don't have an owner."

"The owner of CNN. My boss."

"Oh, Jane Fonda's husband!"

Waters nodded.

Stukey shrugged at the camera and took the phone. "Ted?"

"You sonofabitch," fumed Turner. "You're making a mockery of my network!"

"Drunk again, Ted?" said Stukey.

In fact, Turner had guzzled three very dry martinis with lunch and was full-blown.

Stukey didn't wait for an answer. "It might be your network, but right now it's *my* show. So fuck off, you weenie. Unless you want to send Jane over and let me lick her nipples."

"What? You sonofabitch! I'll come over there myself and . . . !"

"See ya–bye." Stukey plunked the phone down. *"That's* the way to handle bosses," he winked. "Whoooeeee, this is great! I feel like Howard Stern."

The phone rang again.

"Whew, we're hot, Lou. I'll take it." Stukey grabbed the phone from the anchor's grip. "It's probably Jane, wanting her nipples licked." He put the receiver to his ear. "That you, Jane?"

"Willard, it's me, Kyle."

"Not you."

"Willard, we have Arthur Floto standing by."

"Mr. Floto?" Stukey was awed.

"That's right, Willard. He's in Bardstown, Kentucky. We have him on the phone. Arthur?"

"Hi, Willard," said Arthur Floto.

Stukey trembled with goosebumps.

"I just want to tell you I'm sorry," said Floto. He hesitated. "You're a very good artist."

"Very good?" said Stukey.

"Uh, a great artist," said Floto. "You're a great artist, Willard."

"No thanks to you, Mr. Floto. You were a *lousy* teacher."

Floto said nothing.

"You shouldn't have *been* a teacher," Stukey continued. "I bet you became a teacher so you'd have an excuse for hanging around little boys."

"Now wait a minute. . ."

"Because you sure couldn't teach art, that's for damn sure. So it musta been because you're a homo pedophile—ain't that right, Mr. Floto?"

"I don't have to listen to this," shouted Floto. "I'm gonna sue you for slander! *And* CNN!"

"Yeah, sue Ted. He's got a billion dollars to give away."

"Whoa, Arthur . . ." Kyle Pickford interjected.

But Arthur Floto was gone, already dialing his lawyer.

"That was Mr. Arthur Floto." Stukey spoke directly into the camera. "The only thing he knows about art is how to make little boys cry when they don't stick colored mosaic pieces to his ridiculous numbers. A real scumbag homo pedophile."

"Willard? Willard? Are you there?" This was Kyle

Pickford. "Pick up Willard."

Stukey picked up. "Where the hell's my burgoo?"

"It's coming," said Pickford. "We have to fly it down from Kentucky."

"Send enough for everyone," said Stukey.

"How about a hostage?" pushed Pickford.

"Sure, I'd be happy to pop one if you don't get that burgoo here quick." Stukey put the phone down.

62

"COPPA-COPPA-COPPA-FART." This was Jeff Dalkin's reaction to the overwhelming police presence outside One CNN Center in Atlanta.

Nearby, assistant FBI director R. James Cloverland took personal charge of the operation, to the consternation of Atlanta's police chief, who had mayoralty ambitions. But Stukey had crossed state lines and that made it a federal matter.

Lieutenant Pickford reluctantly gave up his mobile phone to Jeff Dalkin, after being directed to do so by Cloverland.

63

THE ANCHOR'S PHONE RANG again, interrupting another Willard Stukey discourse on the value of art over mankind through the ages.

"The only reason we even know what people looked like, acted like and lived like through the centuries is because of art." Stukey ignored the ringing phone. "The only reason we know that prehistoric man existed sixteen thousand years ago is because of paintings he left on limestone walls in caves. Then the French gilders of the twelfth century, the Italian sculptors of the fifteenth century, the English landscape painters of the eighteenth century. Look at da Vinci's *The Last Supper*–whoa, the perspective! Man oh man, the true heroes of history aren't military generals like Napoleon and George Washington. They're Leonardo da Vinci and Michelangelo and Vermeer and van Gogh and Toulouse-Lautrec and . . . goddammit!" Stukey picked up the phone. "What?!"

"Hi, Willard."
"Who's this?"
"It's me. Jeff Dalkin."
"Oh." Stukey paused. "What are *you* doing here?"
"We were supposed to meet. Remember?"
"Oh, yeah, right."
"What happened?"
"Well, I did this instead."
"C'mon, Willard. Let everyone go. This thing's over. Lo mein."
"It's not over."
"Sure it is. I'm right outside, and let me tell you, I've never seen so many friggin' co. . . coppa-coppa-coppa-fart —cops in my life. There's no way out of here."
"Yeah, but I got sixty people in here, at least. Don't that count for nothing?"
"Sure it does," said Dalkin. "That's why they're bringing the burgoo you asked for."
"I'm supposed to give up sixty people for a bowl of burgoo?"
"You got everything you wanted, Willard: A MoMA exhibition, a *New York Times* review, fame, recognition as a great artist. And now they're bringing the burgoo. What else is there?"
"How about an airline ticket to Paris, France?"
"C'mon, Willard. Why would you want to go to Paris?"
"That's where all the great artists go, guy! They appreciate art in Paris, France. They understand it, respect it, not like this country's comic book culture. Yeah, I wanna go live in Paris, France."
"But you killed fifty people, Willard."

"The French don't care about that," said Stukey. "Art and ideas are more important to them. Look at Roman Polanski, the film-maker."

"That was a sex crime," said Dalkin. "Not murder."

"Yeah, okay. Then look at Ira Einhorn."

"Who?"

"The Unicorn. You know, that hippie from Philadelphia who murdered his girlfriend and stashed her in a trunk. The French let Ira stay even though he's guilty of murder. I'll go live with him. He can write, I'll paint."

"Listen, Willard, they'll never let you walk out of here and go to France."

"Then they'll have to kill me. Live on CNN."

"You don't want to die, Willard. Think of all the paintings that won't get painted if you die now."

"Ha! I'm looking at the electric chair, guy. What's the difference?"

"About ten years," said Dalkin. "That's a lot of painting. And you may not get the death penalty. A guy's got to be crazy to do what you're doing. Catch my drift?"

64

A CAULDRON OF BURGOO arrived an hour later. Jeff Dalkin, having elected to deliver it himself, pushed a trolley out of the elevator, into the newsroom.

Stukey rose from the anchor table, weapon in hand. "That my burgoo?" He paused to study Dalkin. "Bruce Willis?"

"No, I'm not Bruce W-W-Willis," Dalkin called across the newsroom. "I'm Jeff Dalkin."

"What?" Stukey was confused. "You think I'm nuts? Is this a fucking movie already?" Stukey looked at Lou Waters for his opinion. "Lou? Is that Bruce Willis or what?"

Lou Waters shrugged. "He looks like Bruce Willis."

Dalkin drew nearer. "I'm not Bruce W-W-Willis, goddammit, lo mein. Do you want your burgoo or not?"

"Yeah, burgoo." Stukey rubbed his hands gleefully. "Bring it on, Bruce. Lou gets to try it first."

"Me?" The anchor's eyes popped.

"Yeah, you, Lou. I gotta make sure they haven't poisoned it. You're the taster."

From behind the camera, Dalkin ladled burgoo into a bowl. "I'm bringing it over," he said. Dalkin walked slowly to the anchor desk and carefully placed the bowl of squirrel brain stew in front of Lou Waters. Then he backed away.

Waters gulped. Perspiration beaded on his forehead. He loosened his tie.

"Go on," prodded Stukey. "Eat."

Waters put spoon to bowl, lifted the spongy, succulent meat to his mouth, and gagged at the smell. "I can't do it!" Waters dropped the spoon. "I'm not eating squirrel brains!"

"Pussy," said Stukey, shaking his head in contempt. "Scoot, man."

"Excuse me?"

"Scoot! Get out! I'm giving your anchor job to someone else."

"But . . ."

"OUT!"

Waters rose quickly and slipped away.

"Yo, Bruce!" Stukey waved his weapon. "C'mon over, guy. You're the new anchor."

Dalkin strode over and took the hot seat next to Stukey.

"Now *you* try the burgoo," Stukey ordered.

Dalkin dipped the spoon into squirrel brain stew, brought it to his mouth, tasted.

"Well?" said Stukey.

"Not bad," said Dalkin. "They should do this at Soup Burg."

"Okay, where's my bowl," snapped the artist. "I'm starved. Lou! Where'd Lou go?"

Waters was slumped in a chair. He sat up. "Huh?"

"Get your fat ass over here, Lou," Stukey commanded. "Serve me my burgoo."

Waters got up, walked to the trolley behind the camera, ladled burgoo into a bowl and delivered it to Stukey.

The artist dug in. "Umm." He slurped and chomped. "Yummy," he muttered. He swallowed. "Shit, this is damn good burgoo."

The phone rang.

"I'm eating." Stukey waved his spoon. "You answer it."

Dalkin picked up. "Yeah?"

"It's Kyle Pickford," announced the police negotiator.

"Coppa-coppa-coppa-fart!" Dalkin touretted. "Ah, shit— Wali of Swat, Wali of Swat, crab cakes, tekka maki. Lo mein!"

Stukey dropped his spoon into the stew and grabbed his gun with both hands. "What the hell's going on? Is that a code for something?"

"No, no," Dalkin put up his palms defensively. "Tourette's."

"Huh?"

"It's a syndrome I suffer."

"You mean, you can't help but cuss like that?"

"Uh-huh."

"Cool." Stukey re-launched himself into burgoo, wolfing it down. He stopped, eyeing Dalkin with new suspicion. "How come I haven't seen this cussing of yours in any movies?"

"Because I'n not Bruce W-W-Willis." Dalkin gritted his teeth. "I'm Jeff Dalkin."

"You're really Jeff Dalkin. My agent?"

Dalkin nodded.

"Okay, I believe you. Where's my bread?"

Dalkin shook his head. "They confiscated it."

"Who did?"

"The F . . . F . . . fucking fatheads from fart-town US-fucking-A–FBI, whew!"

"But it's mine."

Dalkin shrugged. "That's what I told them."

"I'm going to need that money for lawyers," said Stukey. He looked at the camera. "I want it back. I want the paintings from my studio back. I want my paintings from MoMA back. I want everything back." Stukey returned to eating his burgoo. He was quiet, till he finished. Everyone was quiet; a minute of silence. Then Stukey raised his head and faced the camera. "I'm ready to take applications from lawyers," he announced. "I'm looking for the best–a dream team, just like O.J. Gerry Spence? Johnny Cochcrane? Barry Scheck? Any of you guys out there watching? I can pay you guys in art–more money than you've ever dreamed about. It'll be a landmark case: art versus humanity."

The phone rang.

Stukey, excited now, picked up. "Hello?"

"Hi, Willard," said Kyle Pickford.

"Dammit! Get off the phone, Kyle. I'm expecting some lawyers to call."

"Did you like the burgoo, Willard?" asked Pickford.

"Best I ever ate," said Stukey. "I'm going for seconds. Lou?" The artist called out to Lou Waters. "Get another bowl over here, pronto!"

"I've given you what you asked for," said Pickford. "Arthur Floto, burgoo. I think you should release your hostages now."

"And I think I should live in Paris, France," said Stukey.

"No can do," said Pickford. "Leaving here is out of the question. It's time to give yourself up."

"What are you going to give me for killing Mickey Mouse and all those other people?" asked Stukey.

"That's for a judge and jury to decide," said Pickford.

"Okay then, what are you going to give me for *not* killing all the people in this room?"

Pickford was silent.

"Well, Mister Motor-mouth? Huh?" pushed Stukey. "That ought to be worth something?"

"Don't make it worse for yourself, Willard."

"Worse? I've killed over fifty people, guy! Correct me if I'm wrong, Kyle, but doesn't that add up to fifty separate sit-downs in the electric chair or something like a thousand years in prison?"

"Give yourself up, Willard."

"Yeah, yeah—that's easy for you." Stukey glanced around. "What's my phone number here?"

Pickford said nothing.

"I said, what's my number?"

"Why do you. . .?" Pickford began.

"The hell with you." Stukey slammed the phone down. "Lou!" he called out. "What's the number for this friggin' phone?"

Lou Waters recited the number.

"You hear that?" Stukey said to his audience. He repeated the number. "This is the Willard Stukey Call-in Show. Now we're gonna teach Larry King a thing or two."

The phone rang.

"There we go," said Stukey, picking up. "You're live.

Go ahead."

"It's Kyle," said Lieutenant Pickford. "We need to keep this line open."

"The hell we do." Stukey disconnected the hostage negotiator.

The phone rang again.

"You take it," Stukey instructed Dalkin. "And if it's Kyle again, I'm gonna shoot somebody." Stukey raised his weapon.

Dalkin picked up. "Yeah—what?"

"This is Gerry Spence. Is that Willard Stukey?"

"Hold on." Dalkin looked at Stukey. "It's not Kyle. It's that smooth-talking lawyer—lying labonza—with the Buffalo Bill jacket."

"Yeah, I hear. Now we're cooking." Stukey grabbed the receiver. "You gonna represent me, guy?"

"Um, how many paintings do you have?" asked Spence.

"A whole roomful."

"I'm there. Don't talk to anyone till I arrive."

"But I gotta do this show," Stukey protested.

"Do what you must," said Spence. "But once you're in custody, don't say a word. Not one word."

"Thanks, Gerry. You're hired." Stukey cradled the phone.

It rang. Stukey picked up.

"Hello? Hello?" This voice seemed oddly familiar to Jeff Dalkin.

"Is Jeff Dalkin still with you?"

"He *says* he's Jeff Dalkin," said Stukey. "I still think he's Bruce Willis."

"Hang up," said Dalkin.

"Why?" Stukey cupped the phone.

Dalkin shook his head. "Just hang up."

"Bruce or Jeff or whoever he is wants me to hang up on you," Stukey said into the phone.

"That's because he's a crook, a fraud!" blurted Mark Alouwahlia. "I know this man. He takes my money . . ."

"You paid me to do a job," Dalkin faced the camera. "I did it. Burgoo, crab cakes, tekka maki, lo mein."

"You tell me my wife and children are in Perth, Australia," whined Alouwahlia. "I come to Perth, Australia, and they run away again!"

"Yeah, good for them," said Dalkin. "Wali of Swat, Wali of Swat, bootlick from Bangalore. Burgoo, Floto, lo mein."

"You must return my money," wailed Alouwahlia.

"Bite me, wife-beater," said Dalkin. "Crab cakes, tekka maki, lo mein."

Stukey sat back, holding up the phone, bemused by the exchange. "Man, and I thought *I* was nuts."

Alouwahlia was still ranting and raving as Dalkin grabbed the phone and slammed it into the cradle.

A minute later, Stukey fell into a trance-like doze from Xanax, a fast-acting anti-anxiety drug that had been mixed into the burgoo.

"Willard? Willard?" said Dalkin.

But Stukey was catatonic.

Dalkin reached under the anchor desk and grabbed the Hechler & Koch MPSKA4 9mm machine pistol from Stukey's lap. He disengaged the ammunition clip.

"The Willard Stukey Call-in Show is over," declared Dalkin. "Turn that camera off. Lo mein."

65

Willard Stukey was taken into custody by R. James Cloverland, booked and indicted for multiple counts of first-degree murder. A judge quickly dispatched the artist to St. Elizabeth's Hospital in Washington, D.C. for psychiatric evaluation.

Gerry Spence, Stukey's lead defense attorney, immediately filed suit against the FBI, the Museum of Modern Art, and Jeff Dalkin for the return of all Stukey's property.

Dalkin promptly filed suit against Willard Stukey for ten percent of all proceeds from the sale of Stukey's art; Dalkin also filed suit against the Walt Disney Company and Michael Eisner for unfair dismissal, and for two million dollars, the reward offered by Disney for the apprehension of Willard Stukey.

Arthur Floto filed suit against Willard Stukey and CNN for slander.

Mark Alouwahlia, who never found his wife and children, filed suit against Dalkin, demanding the return of one million dollars, plus punitive damages, and for slander;

Dalkin counter-sued.

Lucy Dengrove of Charleston, South Carolina, filed suit against Dalkin and Alouwahlia for invasion of privacy and computer theft.

The families of Walt Disney World murder victims filed a class action suit against the Walt Disney Company for failing to adequately protect their loved ones on Disney property.

And the widowed Macula Drabowski filed suit against the FBI for the unjustified homicide of her deaf-mute husband, Morton Drabowski, at Hobby Lobby in Santa Fe, New Mexico.

66

OLIVIA SQUALLACE WAS THE FIRST to sign a book contract, extracting a tidy advance of one hundred thousand dollars from Doubleday & Company for her role in the Stukey drama.

Arthur Floto was next to score a book deal: a coffee-table book on mosaic-making.

On Willard Stukey's behalf, Gerry Spence negotiated a five million dollar book publishing and TV movie tie-in with Random House and Castle Rock Entertainment, the proceeds of which would be distributed equally between victims injured in Stukey's attacks and the art department of the New School for Social Research in New York City, minus Spence's hefty commission for representing Stukey on a contingency basis.

Rex Lappin sold the portrait of himself sketched by Willard Stukey to MoMA for seventy-five-thousand dollars. He spent the money on tuition at Columbia's School of Journalism, became a reporter for *The National Enquirer*, and was assigned the Bruce Willis beat.

Stukey's asshole sketch of Saddam Hussein was put to auction at Sotheby's. It sold for sixty-nine-thousand dollars to pop-star Elton John.

Shareholders of the Walt Disney Company voted to revoke Michael Eisner's annual bonus of share options totalling millions of dollars and utilize those funds to purchase a state-of-the-art security system for Disney's theme parks.

Such security, however, could not prevent a tornado from twisting through EPCOT, trashing eleven nations and planting a mock Eiffel Tower into the roof of Disney's Yacht Club Resort.

67

WILLARD STUKEY WAS DIAGNOSED with mad squirrel disease, which, like mad cow disease, caused Creutzfeldt-Jakob disease. Even though a CAT scan illustrated that Creutzfeldt-Jakob had cratered the left side of Stukey's brain, the judge presiding over his trial refused to accept an insanity plea.

Stukey was found guilty on all counts of first-degree murder and sentenced to death by electrocution. He was ordered to the State Penitentiary in Starke, Florida.

Eight years later, two days before Stukey was scheduled to die on the electric chair, Gerry Spence invoked a Supreme Court ruling on capital punishment stipulating that "the condemned has to be aware of his execution and he has to know why he is being executed."

Alas, Stukey's brain had been so shrunken by Creutzfeld-Jakob, that the artist no longer knew who he was, let alone why he faced execution, or even what execution meant.

When Willard Stukey finally succumbed to mad squirrel disease one year later, the Animal Liberation Front adopted the squirrel as their international symbol of animals fighting back against humankind.

68

After years and years, all litigation was resolved, enriching numerous lawyers.

Eventually, everyone died. Life went on.

Three hundred years later, Willard Stukey was recognized as the greatest artist of his time.

Lo mein.

CORINTHIAN BOOKS

Write your own book review!

We love to hear from our readers and pass along all the reivews to the author. Tell us what you liked. Tell us what moved you. Tell us what you found most provocative!

Send your reviews to Corinthian Books, P.O. Box 1898, Mt. Pleasant SC 29465 USA or e-mail them to:

Reviews@Corinthianbooks.com